The Dragons of Incendium

WYVERN'S OUTLAW

DEBORAH COOKE

AUTHOR OF *WYVERN'S WARRIOR*

ISBN: 978-1-988479-39-2

Chapter One

nguissa, dragon princess and Captain of the starship Archangel, didn't make mistakes.

That was the reason she'd survived almost three hundred years of roaming the galaxy with the strategy of following only the rules that suited her.

Yet, she had apparently just made a colossal mistake, one for which her sister Thalina would pay the price.

It was impossible.

And obviously true.

Anguissa scowled. She checked the ship's position after the jump, recalculated and reviewed. She hadn't chosen this quadrant as a destination, yet here they were. She didn't like this quadrant or know it well—it had always given her a bad feeling, even on the star charts, and she'd visited it only once.

It was widely believed to be the hunting ground of the Gloria Furore, the notorious space pirates who would steal anyone or anything. They sold to the highest bidder.

Anguissa had also survived as a star pilot by not provoking the Gloria Furore.

That she was back in the identical location as that single visit defied belief, especially as she hadn't chosen it as a destination. The presence of the Armada Seven, a ship commanded by Captain Hellemut, made her location indisputable.

The nav system didn't show that Anguissa had made a mistake. In fact, it indicated that she had chosen an entirely different destination, the one she remembered choosing, half a galaxy away from here.

Which could only mean that her ship had been sabotaged.

Captain Hellemut had somehow compelled Anguissa to come back.

It was all too easy to remember the words of the captain allied with the Gloria Furore, intergalactic bandits of the worst kind.

To appear in this quadrant once could be an accident, Captain Anguissa. To appear twice would be a provocation.

There wasn't a whole lot of doubt about how this would play out. Any second now, Hellemut would hail the Archangel—if she didn't attack first.

Anguissa needed to keep Hellemut from firing, given the payload still locked in the hold of the Archangel. It was secured and quarantined, but destroying the Archangel would disperse it.

Which was the last thing Anguissa wanted to happen.

She hid her trepidation from both her sister Thalina and the android who Thalina insisted was the Carrier of her Seed.

"You said this sector would be vacant," the android noted. Powers of observation were probably supposed to be a benefit of his kind but it was one of the traits that Anguissa found really irritating.

She hoped it irked him that she called him "Robot."

Anguissa tapped the display and spoke lightly, as if she wasn't panicking inside. "That's the problem with a quick departure."

"Where are we?" Thalina asked.

"Where we shouldn't be," Anguissa admitted. "I called up a list of recently visited locations and chose the wrong one. We're too far out. Frack. I don't usually make these kinds of mistakes."

Thalina's voice rose. "But we can get to Cumae, right?"

"There are sufficient stores for one life form to reach Cumae or to return to Incendium," the android said. "Not both."

"That makes no sense," Thalina protested.

"Our present location is distant from both planets," he informed her. He drew a triangle in the air, one with a long point. "Consider that we are here." He indicated the single point. "To jump to one or the other is a difference of direction more than distance." He tapped. "That said, the individual would have several days of minimal nourishment if Incendium was chosen as destination, but would still arrive alive."

Anguissa barely listened. She didn't need the lesson. She was thinking about fuel.

Strategy.

And a virulent virus locked in the hold.

Thalina was convinced that the android was the Carrier of the Seed, the destined father of her child, and might be her HeartKeeper. That was insane, to Anguissa's thinking, but she respected her sister's conclusions.

She could smell Thalina's reaction to the Seed, against every expectation. It must somehow be true.

Anguissa had to ensure her sister's safety, whether she was pregnant or not.

The upside was that Anguissa suspected Captain Hellemut really wanted her and no one else. It was a personal lesson Hellemut intended to give, which meant it might be possible to send the Archangel out of reach.

Anguissa decided to teach the captain of the Armada Seven to be careful what she wished for.

It was possible, after all, that Captain Hellemut didn't

know that Anguissa was a dragon shifter. She wasn't rumored to be strong on research, and Anguissa hadn't revealed her true nature in their last encounter. She *might* have the element of surprise on her side.

It was only fair, since she'd been surprised herself. Who had tampered with the nav system of the Archangel? Who had betrayed her?

Who had dared?

It was a mystery she hoped she had the luxury of time to solve.

Thalina and her android were talking, but Anguissa hadn't really been listening. "Not to interrupt you two, but we've got more trouble than supplies," she said. She pushed her sister firmly down and out of sight. There was no telling what else had been tampered with. There might be a video feed to the Armada Seven, as well. "I know that ship." She pointed to the display on the far side of the deck, which showed the Armada Seven in all its hideous glory.

It was an ugly ship, manufactured for power and not for grace, then repaired as necessary in foreign ports. It was large and grey, a freighter later armed for war, but not a vessel to be underestimated. It had enough firepower to annihilate the Archangel five times over.

"We are being hailed," the android said. "By the other ship in the quadrant."

"By Captain Hellemut of the Armada Seven," Anguissa agreed.

"You anticipated this meeting?" he asked.

"No, but I recognize the ship and I know its captain well enough to speculate on her plans."

"Ah!" he said.

There was only one way to get Thalina safely away from Captain Hellemut and the android was Anguissa's best chance of an ally.

"Okay, this is what's going to happen, Robot, and

you're going to make it so." Anguissa leaned toward Acion and gave him rapid instructions to flee with Thalina after she teleported to the Armada Seven herself alone.

"This is illogical," he protested.

She glared at him. "On the contrary, it's the only thing that makes sense," she insisted, then took advantage of what had to be his basic programming. "You exist to serve right?"

"Correct."

"And I'm your captain, so I command you to do this in order to defend my sister."

He frowned and Anguissa wished he could calculate probabilities a little faster. She was well aware of the flashing signal on the comm and she knew that Captain Hellemut's reactions wouldn't be improved by delay.

"What's happening?" Thalina asked.

Anguissa glared at her sister. "Stay out of view and keep silent if you want to live. You do *not* want to mess with these people."

"Who are they?"

"Frack knows but they work for the Gloria Furore."

That was apparently all the warning her sister needed because she hid immediately.

"And strap down," Anguissa added in a growl.

"This is excellent advice," the android said and Anguissa breathed a sigh of relief that he was going to do as instructed.

"And you will ensure that my sister has no opportunity to become curious about the contents of the hold," she muttered in an undertone.

"I note that it's secured and quarantined," the android said.

"And there's only one person in the universe who could figure out my code."

Their gazes met and held for a moment, then the

android nodded agreement.

It wouldn't take Thalina long to deduce what Anguissa was planning either, so Anguissa didn't give her any time. She went to the transport deck, propping her hands on her hips as she faced the screen. "Open the frequency to hail, Robot." she commanded. "Let's do this thing. Oxygen is wasting."

The screen was immediately filled with the sight of Captain Hellemut in all her hideous three-eyed glory. She had to be the most unattractive creature in twenty sectors, but Anguissa smiled. "Greetings, Captain Hellemut," she said in the universal tongue. "How I have missed the sunshine of your smile."

"You are a fool to return, Captain Anguissa," Captain Hellemut replied with a smirk. "And I thought you were clever."

"I just dislike unfinished business," Anguissa said.

"The Archangel is targeted by all of our weapons, Captain Anguissa. You are in no position to negotiate."

"What do you want?"

"Complete surrender, of course."

"Is that all?"

"You, first, and then the Archangel."

How deep did the sabotage go in the Archangel's systems? Would the ship surrender itself to Hellemut, regardless of what Anguissa commanded?

She still couldn't think of how it had been done. Someone on her own crew must have betrayed her, but Anguissa couldn't imagine who it might have been. She kept her crew small, on purpose, and they'd all been with her for a long time. She trusted them.

Could Hellemut have somehow compromised the nav system at a distance?

Was there a worm lurking in the communication link? Anguissa didn't think that was possible, but she would hurry the conversation just in case it had become possible.

Thalina had to escape.

"And if I decline this generous offer?" she asked.

"I'll obliterate you both together, right now."

"How very persuasive you are, Captain Hellemut." Anguissa raised her hands. "Open a beam to transport me to your deck so I can surrender in person."

Hellemut chuckled, evidently not realizing that Anguissa never surrendered anything this easily. It was an advantage and Anguissa would take it. She gave a nod to the android, then turned her head to wink at Thalina so that the other captain couldn't see.

Then she felt the tingle of the transport. It always started with the hair on the back of her neck standing up and a shiver rolling over her flesh. She had to arrive in the same form as she departed, but that wouldn't last long. The tingle claimed her, the transport dividing her molecules and flinging them along the trajectory to the Armada Seven.

Anguissa vaguely felt a void open behind her, a hint that the Archangel had jumped just as she'd commanded, then the heat that she always felt on emergence.

She felt the deck of the Armada Seven beneath her feet and didn't waste a second. She summoned the shift, changed shape, and breathed a torrent of dragon fire directly at Captain Hellemut.

In that same instant, Anguissa smelled the Seed. It sent a jolt of desire through her, a primal urge to mate that was so hot and imperative that nothing else mattered except identifying the Carrier and seducing him completely.

Hellemut screamed and evicted her seat to hide behind it. The seat burned, flames dancing high, and the air filled with smoke. Instead of finishing what she'd started, Anguissa scanned the deck, inhaling deeply.

The Carrier of the Seed was the co-pilot, the man

who was staring at her with narrowed eyes. He was tall and muscular, a man who could have been from Incendium—except that Anguissa had never yearned to claim a man from Incendium so badly. His expression was guarded and his aura was dark.

She realized with a start that he was an *umbro*, a species from Centurios feared and loathed throughout the known universe. They were often called Soul-Stealers. They captured and claimed, leaving their victims to bleed to death while they hunted anew.

Anguissa took another breath of the Seed and didn't care.

She wanted him.

She wanted him now.

And he was hers to possess.

Ryke knew better than to waste opportunity.

Although he was tempted to linger, just to witness the arrival of Princess Anguissa on the deck of the Armada Seven. He wondered if she could possibly look as alluring in reality as she did on the display—some captains did manipulate their appearance—and he wouldn't have minded having a closer view. Even on the display, her bold stance was enough to take his breath away—never mind the curves straining her uniform in all the right places and her dark eyes flashing with defiance. He was curious about women with spirit and verve, as they were unknown on Centurios. Ryke had a feeling Anguissa was both.

And that she would more than satisfy his curiosity.

He also guessed she would quickly shift shape to her dragon form upon arrival, and that would be a sight to behold. He'd never seen a dragon shifter and was curious why they were so despised on his home planet. They had to dangerous, of course, but at the same time, it would be exciting to survive an encounter with one.

But even this temptation wasn't enough for him to compromise his own plans. Ryke had been waiting too long for a chance to escape. Beautiful women and the temptation they offered had been his downfall in the past. A long run of enforced celibacy couldn't influence his choices, not now.

He needed to to grab the opportunity Anguissa offered. He'd never seen Hellemut so driven to conquer a foe before.

Was it personal?

Did that matter? It was *useful*, and that was all that should be important to Ryke.

As soon as the sight of Anguissa faded on the display, Ryke watched his superior. Captain Hellemut leaned forward and gripped her chair, her anticipation palpable.

Her attention was completely fixed on the transport deck.

Was this the real Captain Hellemut or one of her doppelgangers? The copies had been improving so steadily that Ryke couldn't reliably tell the difference any more.

It didn't matter, really. He just needed to remember that there were at least two Hellemuts to escape.

Ryke could feel the tingle on his nape, the one he always felt during a transport—whether he was witnessing it or participating in it. Any second, Anguissa would arrive.

After that, Hellemut would survey the deck.

She didn't miss a lot with her three eyes.

This was a once-in-captivity opportunity.

Ryke slowly eased away from his station. The trick was not to catch Hellemut's attention with a sudden movement. His heart was pounding and his palms were damp. He hoped his concern didn't trigger any sensors set to monitor anxiety in the crew. He kept his hands away from the controls, just in case. Most of the crew looked to be a bit worried so maybe his reaction wouldn't stand out.

There was a shimmer above the transport deck. Hellemut lifted a finger and leaned closer.

Ryke ducked. He heard the slight sound of Anguissa's arrival and felt the air change. He guessed she was changing shape, because his ears popped, but he was on the move. He expected her to roast Hellemut, which would suit him just fine.

He felt heat and heard a roar. He smelled burning flesh.

Everything was exactly as he'd expected.

Ryke raced across the deck, taking advantage of the distraction Anguissa offered. The rest of the crew appeared to be transfixed by the sight. The color drained from the face of Lored, the nav specialist, when Ryke was alongside him.

Lored had seen a lot.

Lored swore softly under his breath, clearly amazed by Anguissa.

It was too much. Ryke couldn't deny himself one glimpse. He was on the threshold of escape, almost free, when he dared to glance back.

Then he stared as well.

Anguissa was magnificent.

In dragon form, she was obsidian, gleaming black, with a writhing mane of hair instead of the scales he might have expected down her spine. She filled the transport deck, her back against the ceiling, her tail coiled across the floor and into the command area. Her eyes had orange flames instead of pupils, as if she was filled with fire, even as she exhaled a torrent of flames at Captain Hellemut.

Hellemut had ducked behind her massive chair. The flames appeared around it like a corona, but Hellemut was looking over the deck.

Ryke should have defended his captain.

He wanted to help with her demise, instead.

Anguissa seemed to be doing a good job. Time to run.

"Ryke!" Hellemut snapped. He froze and straightened, knowing he'd been caught and doubting the result would be good. "Why have you left your post?"

Anguissa stopped breathing flames as her attention shifted to him. Having her gaze fixed upon him was both terrifying and exciting—in fact, he hadn't been so aroused in years. Celibacy definitely didn't agree with him. It was messing with his concentration. Anguissa inhaled and Ryke was sure she'd breathe more fire. She took a step closer, her eyes gleaming, even as he eased back.

The deck shook under her weight.

"Ryke?" his captain demanded.

Ryke bowed low to Hellemut, pretending to be frightened. "I left my post because there's a dragon, Captain. It seemed sensible to flee."

Hellemut sneered. "And you, a warrior of Centurios, are afraid? Have we finally found something to terrify you, Ryke?"

"I've never seen a dragon, Captain." He glanced at Anguissa and summoned an expression of disgust. "They're filthy abominations."

Anguissa reared up and roared, her eyes blazing so brilliantly that they were like glimpses of an inferno. The dark mane rippled on her back as if it was a living organism itself. Ryke realized it was a line of snakes, snakes with eyes as yellow as those of the dragon. They bared their fangs as she scattered sparks across the deck, then she took a deep breath, obviously intending to loose another blast at Hellemut.

"There will be repercussions for this insubordination, Ryke," Hellemut snarled, even as she reached over to his station and loosed the beams aimed at the transport deck. They generated an energy field of tangled green light, a vortex that surrounded and contained the dragon. It was designed to halt a hostile invasion from the transport deck and its effectiveness sickened him. Ryke could smell dragon scales burning as the trap closed around Anguissa like a net and she snarled as she was bound.

The ship shook when she fell motionless to the transport deck. A shudder rolled through her massive body as her eyes closed.

She looked dead.

Turned out that subduing a dragon was very easy.

Ryke felt his suspicion rise.

Too easy.

Captain Anguissa, he remembered from his research, was inclined to use a feint in battle.

"That's right," Hellemut mused as she reseated herself in her chair. She brushed imaginary dirt from her sleeves, settling her enormous mass in place with satisfaction. "You have little tolerance of non-humanoid species on Centurios. I had forgotten." She beckoned with one massive hand. "Exterminate the abomination, Ryke. You might enjoy it as much as I will."

"Yes, Captain."

Hellemut waved at the fallen Anguissa, whose eyes were open just a slit. "Farewell, Princess Anguissa. I don't doubt that you're still listening. I regret that we didn't have longer to enjoy each other's company but really, I thought you'd give a better fight than this." She glanced back at the crew and her voice sharpened. "I expect damage reports as soon as the worm has breathed her last."

Ryke hesitated, trying to figure out how to foil Hellemut.

He didn't want to see Anguissa die.

And he certainly didn't want to be the one

responsible for the deed. It was one thing to be abducted by the Gloria Furore—it had to be quite another to have a league of dragon warriors from Incendium hunting him, intending to take their vengeance for the death of one of their royal family.

Hellemut watched, eyes glittering, as Ryke returned to his station and surveyed the console. Why hadn't Anguissa changed shape again? He glanced up and discovered that she was watching him. He could see the fire burning in the narrow slits of her eyes.

It wasn't dimmed at all.

Her nostrils quivered and her eyes shone, those snakes trembling, as if she was excited about something.

She had to be pretending to be more subdued than she was.

Maybe all she needed was a chance.

He held her gaze and the snakes bared their fangs. They were odd, but evidently a good clue to her thoughts.

If given that opportunity, Anguissa would create the distraction Ryke needed to escape. She'd take her vengeance upon one version of Hellemut and he'd run. Ryke smiled and let his hand hover over the controls.

"Say your prayers, Snake-Eyes," he said, his words prompting Hellemut's chuckle.

Anguissa's eyes flashed. Did she understand his plan? Ryke had to hope so. He tapped a command, knowing Hellemut could see it on her own display.

She watched, then smiled and settled back, anticipating a show. "Excellent choice, Ryke. A slow incineration will maximize my pleasure."

As soon as Hellemut averted her gaze, Ryke changed the command to one that would stop the beams and release Anguissa. He executed it before he could be stopped.

The force field blinked out, the green net of energy

disappearing before their eyes.

"Ryke! What have you done?" Hellemut had time to roar before Anguissa's answering bellow filled the deck with deafening sound.

He should have run, but Ryke had to watch.

A dragon princess was a dangerous temptation.

In the blink of an eye, Anguissa was on her feet and bounding toward the console that had emitted the energy beams. She ripped it from its mooring and cast it across the deck so that it shattered and smashed. Ryke ducked and retreated as she incinerated the crew that stepped up to retaliate, her plume of flame frying the wall containing the nav console to blackened wreckage.

The Armada Seven had just become space debris.

There was no better time to leave, to Ryke's thinking.

Hellemut shouted commands in fury but Anguissa turned the wall of fire upon her once again. Hellemut's scream rose higher in her anguish. A pane of glass popped due to the frequency of the sound and the crew ducked as shards scattered over them.

Alarms sounded even as Ryke was filled with satisfaction.

It was good to see Hellemut suffer.

It would be better to know that she was dead. She appealed to him, stretching out one hand from the core of the flames. Ryke simply stared back, letting her see that he wouldn't help her.

Mercy had no place in their relationship. She'd taught him that.

Fury lit her eyes but Ryke didn't care.

It was payback time.

The other crew members just watched, too. A lack of loyalty was, Ryke supposed, a hazard of creating a crew by abduction and keeping them in their place with physical torture.

Hellemut's screams faded as the smell of burning

flesh became oppressive. When the flames stopped, a cacophony of alarms made him want to plug his ears. The sprinkler system had activated itself and the water made electrical systems short. Sparks flew across the deck, igniting fires where they landed. Anguissa shredded the captain of the Armada Seven with her talons, cast her aside, and scanned the deck hungrily.

The realization that she wasn't satisfied hit the crew like an icy tide of shock. The deck filled with shouts and chaos. When one crew member reached for the comm, Anguissa swung her tail and smashed the communications console, sending a chunk crashing to the floor. There was a small explosion, then eruptions of brilliant light all over the deck.

Ryke saw the nav specialist, Lored, lunge for the button that would awaken the sleeping troops. Better late than never.

He realized that even this opportunity was dissolving before his eyes. The temptation of beauty had almost cost him a high price again.

The Armada Seven shuddered, as if it mourned the passing of Hellemut—Ryke supposed someone should—then began to slowly spin. Crew members staggered as the propulsion that kept a modicum of gravity on the deck failed in spurts.

He lunged for the portal, fearing he'd waiting too long.

"Ryke of Centurios!" Anguissa shouted, stepping on the corpse of Hellemut.

He froze, his blood running cold that he was the object of her attention.

Could a dragon smile? It seemed to Ryke that she did as she approached him, and he feared the worst. With another sweep of her tail, Anguissa cleared the deck, smashing the team into the walls. She spewed more flame over the survivors as if disinterested in their fates, her eyes gleaming as she stared at him.

"I seize command of the Armada Seven, which means you all answer to me." Her voice was low and sexy, somehow feminine despite her dragon form.

Ryke really had been alone too long.

But she was so magnificent.

So beautiful, in either form.

His mouth went dry.

He held her gaze, even as she breathed a stream of fire that roasted the tips of his boots. "Not me," he dared to say.

Her eyes shone. "Yet you stopped at my summons, even though you think me an abomination," she mused, smoke rising from her nostrils.

"On Centurios, all non-human life forms are considered abominations," Ryle said in a matter-of-fact tone.

"Why?"

"Because the bestial mind is different," he confessed. Time was slipping away. The troops had to be awakening in the storage hold far below. Ryke heard the airlocks groan and recognized that the damaged deck would be sealed off from the rest of the ship before it was further compromised.

"More focused?" Anguissa demanded, eyes blazing. He could feel the force of her will upon him and averted his gaze.

"More manipulative." He bit out the words, seeing her skepticism. He elaborated to insult her, hoping she would turn away from him. "A beast can deny the will of an *umbro*, twist the truth and even deceive the *umbro* into believing he'd witnessed something that had never happened. Such abominations defy the rules and refuse to be controlled. That added to their tendency to deceive means they had to be exterminated."

Her eyes flashed. "We're not on Centurios, Ryke."

She was already showing her true nature, her interest compelling him to stand and explain when he should have been running.

"No. We're in deep shit, Snake-Eyes." He gestured to the smoking and charred remains of the ship's controls. "If you're taking command of this pile of junk, good luck with it."

"Not a fan of the Armada Seven, Ryke?"

"Trashing the nav system was a short-sighted strategy if you'd meant to use this vessel to go anywhere at all. What is your exit plan?"

She was surprised. Ryke guessed it was because of his form of address, not because of the situation. She had to know that trashing the deck would have repercussions.

She couldn't be stupid, could she? That would have been a real abomination.

"You're impertinent, Ryke."

"I'm honest, Snake-Eyes. It's a novelty around here."

"And you're an *umbro*," she whispered, leaning closer. Her eyes glittered. "Why haven't you killed them all?" Her voice dropped low. "Why haven't you killed me?"

"There are some places even an *umbro* doesn't want to go." He wasn't going to explain his strategy, not to a dragon shifter.

Her eyes narrowed and he wondered how sharp her hearing was. Could she hear the airlocks and the troops?

Ryke could. The airlock over his head was moving and would slide into place in seconds. The deck would be sealed off and the damage contained until it could be assessed and repaired. Either way, the Armada Seven wasn't going anywhere soon.

He had to leave immediately and forget this dragon princess.

"It's been a treat, Fire Breath," he said, and waved before he ran. Ryke took a chance that she wouldn't be able to respond quickly enough to stop him, but he feared it was a long shot.

Even with the air lock closing.

"Stop!" Anguissa cried.

Ryke didn't.

• • •

The Seed.

The scent of it filled Anguissa with a seductive mix of yearning and satisfaction. Her lust was raw and rampant, her need so potent that it made her a little bit dizzy. The scent of the Seed made her desire rise and obliterated every other concern from her mind.

It was dangerous and irresistible.

It even overwhelmed her aversion to *umbros*.

She knew what Ryke was, but she still wanted him. That was amazing. He was tall and strong, a warrior among men, and—if he hadn't been an *umbro*—Anguissa would have wanted him even without the encouragement of the Seed.

But he was an *umbro*. She should know better.

Ryke. A good strong name.

She could readily believe that he was from Centurios, whose fighting men were legendary throughout the galaxy for their ruthlessness, their cunning, and their raw power. That he was an *umbro* should have given her pause, but the Seed allowed for no hesitation. She was looking forward to claiming him, no matter what price she had to pay.

It was true that the Seed had surprised her and made her flow of dragon fire falter. It was true that she'd been a little distracted as she tried to identify him in the ranks of the crew. It was definitely true that she'd been more enthusiastic in breathing fire than would have been ideal. It was the Seed, undermining her judgment, obliterating all concerns beyond seducing the Carrier.

But once she'd spotted Ryke, she'd let herself be captured, knowing she needed to reserve her strength for their mating.

He'd not only criticized her technique—which was refreshing—but he'd facilitated her release.

Clearly, their thoughts were as one. She hadn't believed he was revolted by her nature. No, there had been a very interested gleam in his eyes, one that Anguissa recognized well. She liked his blunt speech and his audacity.

Why was he running?

Belatedly, Anguissa recalled what she should have realized all along. The Seed was turning her into an idiot. Of course, Ryke was right. The deck would be cordoned off from the rest of the ship since it had been damaged. Her passionate extinction of Hellemut had compromised the Armada Seven more than she should have dared.

But Ryke had a plan.

He knew the ship better than she did, and she trusted him.

He was the Carrier of the Seed, after all.

This line of thought took less than seconds.

Anguissa shifted shape on the way across the deck, reaching the portal he'd used in her human form. She seized a weapon from a wounded guard, striking him in the face to startle him into releasing it. Even in her smaller form, she had to roll beneath the closing airlock to escape before it was sealed.

Half a dozen crew members had managed to escape, but Anguissa fired on them and they backed away. Most were already wounded and none would survive long. She doubted this one was the only air lock that would be secured. There'd be at least one more that was automatically deployed, if not two. Anyone on the wrong side of the air lock when it sealed, would die quickly.

She saw Ryke ahead of her, running down the corridor, though she could have found him by the scent of the Seed alone. She galloped in pursuit, encouraged to greater speed by the promise of their union.

It would be fast and furious the first time. She didn't have the patience for leisure. She wanted him. She wanted the Seed. She needed him immediately. There was no possible question of a delay.

Anguissa even considered the merit of a small, non-critical injury, maybe to the ankle, just to slow Ryke down, then decided against it.

She wanted him whole. Perfect.

And she was gaining on him.

She leaped as he reached the end of the corridor and caught him around the waist, the force of her impact sending them both sprawling on the floor of the lurching ship. The Armada Seven rolled in that moment, clearly experiencing a greater failure of its gravity generators, and the floor became the ceiling.

Anguissa used the momentum to land on top of Ryke so they were chest to chest. He felt good, all hard muscle and masculinity. She smiled at him as she framed his face in her hands. They were essentially alone, the crew members on this side of the air lock staying out of sight.

"How long until the Gloria Furore sends reinforcements?" she murmured.

His gaze flicked, his pulse leaping beneath her touch. She felt his erection against her thighs and smiled at the unmistakable sign of his enthusiasm. She'd been right. The attraction *was* mutual.

Ryke surveyed her, then locked his hands around her waist and drew her closer in a most satisfactory way.

They *were* thinking as one! The smell of the Seed invaded Anguissa's senses, tempting her, beguiling her, driving every other thought from her mind.

This might be the fastest seduction ever.

It might also be the most satisfying one.

"Their nearest ship is at the far end of the sector." Ryke was obviously calculating. Anguissa liked that her touch seemed to be distracting him. She brushed her lips across his, savoring how he shivered, liking how he tasted. He had a short beard, just a day or two of growth, long enough to be soft, dark enough to make him look dangerous. "Roughly a month, in Incendium terms."

"Good," Anguissa purred, running her hands over his hard strength. "I always feel celebratory after I survive certain death."

He lifted a brow. "You do it that often, Snake-Eyes?"

"All the time," she confessed. "Danger is the spice of life."

Ryke smiled, looking confident, cocky and sexy enough to eat. His voice dropped low. "There are other spices I prefer."

"Like?"

"Like survival." He rolled her to her back in the same moment that he captured her lips with his own. It was a good kiss. A great kiss. A kiss so thorough and proprietary that it left Anguissa burning for more. It certainly distracted her from whatever nonsense he'd said. She raised her hand to grip his hair and pull him closer, but Ryke pushed abruptly to his feet.

By the time she opened her eyes, he'd claimed her weapon and shoved it into his belt. He gave her that little wave again, then turned to run in the same direction again.

"Survival?" she echoed, suspecting she'd missed something.

"That's the one." Ryke touched a fingertip to his ear with a short glance back, then ran faster.

Anguissa straightened and listened. She heard the distant vibration of many feet.

Marching in unison.

Soldiers, within the ship and coming toward the deck.

She swore and scrambled to her feet, once again running in pursuit of Ryke. "You said it would be a month!"

"It will be," he countered. "The soldiers in the hold don't take that long to awaken, though."

"In the hold?"

"Cyborgs, kept chilled to slow their metabolisms. They breathe less, eat less and live longer that way. There are three chambers of them, just waiting to be revived."

Anguissa almost growled. "I hate robots."

"Technically, robots aren't androids..."

"Spare me the lecture. I know the differences. I don't like any of them."

"Tell me what you really think."

Anguissa glared at him. "You define abomination your way and I'll define it mine. Who revived them?"

"Someone on deck. I saw the resuscitate command given."

"Shouldn't they have been awakened before the battle began?"

He granted her an amused glance. "It appears that Hellemut underestimated you, Princess."

"Is that why you helped me escape?"

"No. I helped you escape to help myself escape," he replied as he came to a halt before a sealed portal. The sound of the footfalls was louder and Anguissa glanced behind them. She heard Ryke tap a code into the panel beside a locked door.

"You mean you're not one of the Gloria Furore?"

"Bite your tongue," he chided. "I'm slave labor, or I have been until just now." The door slid open, revealing a yawning darkness. Anguissa took a deep breath and guessed that they were moving closer to the hold. The air was colder and smelled faintly of metal and fuel.

"But they don't let anybody go. Those troops are coming..."

"If we're caught, I'll just tell them you captured me."

The door closed behind them, sealing them in a dark

corridor as Anguissa laughed lightly. "They'll never believe it."

Ryke held up a small light. It shone beneath his face, giving him a sinister appearance. He dropped his voice to a whisper. "The surveillance film of your arrival will have been downloaded to them so that they can prepare for your destruction," he confided. "They'll believe it."

Anguissa glanced down the corridor. "What makes you think you can just leave?"

"I made all the preparations." He gave her a hot look. "The Gloria Furore fucked up, Snake-Eyes. They trusted me and I took advantage of their mistake." Ryke looked determined and grim, as well as a bit reckless.

Umbros were predators, destroyers, said to have no moral code. Anguissa shivered, because she wanted him so badly.

The footsteps were louder.

Anguissa tried to ignore the distraction of the Seed and pretty much failed. "And what about me? Should I trust you, Ryke?"

"That's entirely up to you. I'm leaving and there's room for one more if you want to come along."

"You're inviting me?"

He winced. "I have a weakness for beautiful women." He shook his head, apparently surprised by his own words. "Even the ones are a lot of trouble."

Anguissa felt herself smile. "That sounds like an invitation I can't refuse." She ran her hand over his shoulder and felt his breath catch in response. "Don't worry, Ryke. I'll make it worth your while."

Again, his gaze collided with hers, the intensity in his eyes making her heart skip. "I know." He nodded to the open portal. "Now, move. There won't be any second chances."

CHAPTER TWO

Anguissa moved, glad that someone was thinking clearly when the Seed was jumbling her own thoughts. She couldn't tell whether the corridor inclined downward or the ship's shifting gravity just made it seem that way, but it didn't matter. She hurried along its length, grabbing hand rungs as necessary to haul herself along it.

When she realized Ryke wasn't right behind her, she looked back in time to see him fry the security panel of the door they'd just passed through.

An alarm went off.

"Now, who's not planning ahead?" she muttered under her breath.

"They know where we are anyway," Ryke replied, vaulting past her. Their bodies collided for a moment that sent fire through Anguissa's veins, then he was hurrying ahead. "The best I can do is defend our head start, Snake-Eyes."

Anguissa hoped it would be long enough.

He leaped into the darkness ahead, showing a familiarity in his surroundings that Anguissa didn't share. When she heard him collide with some surface, she guessed they were near the end of the corridor.

Probably another air lock.

She was right. Ryke tried to unlock the next portal

but his code was declined. He muttered a curse, then fired at the control panel, roasting it. He tried to kick open the door, but this one was an air lock and of heavier gauge.

"Stand back," Anguissa said. She shifted shape and breathed fire, even as the sounds of pursuit became louder. The metal melted and fused so that Ryke backed away from the heat. She kicked it out with one foot, then shifted shape again to fit through it.

"One less air lock," Ryke muttered.

"Too bad for whoever needs to breathe," Anguissa agreed.

She didn't imagine that he ran faster then. At the end of this shorter corridor, there were space suits secured to the wall.

They had to be moving into a zone that granted access to the small Starpods moored to the outside of the freighter.

She reached for one of the suits, but Ryke waved her onward. "No time!" he said as there was a crash from far behind them.

She eyed him, knowing that they'd be even more vulnerable. "Don't screw up."

The flash of his irreverent grin both surprised and encouraged her. The sight made the call of the Seed even more imperative. She told herself she should count herself lucky that Ryke's smile was gone all too soon. "I thought adventure was the spice of life, Snake-Eyes," he murmured, eyes glinting. "Don't you like adventures?"

"I don't like screw-ups."

"And ripping out the nav console doesn't count?" Ryke didn't wait for an answer, which was good because there wasn't time to explain to him about the Seed. Even as she ran for her life, Anguissa wanted to pull him to a stop and touch him. The Seed was dangerous. He swung open the hatch and they slipped through it, then he closed and locked it behind them.

"Keep going!" he said, still tapping into the console.

Anguissa did as he instructed.

"They didn't find that one," he muttered with satisfaction as he caught up to her.

There was no time to ask. Judging by the sounds behind them, they needed every advantage they could get.

A pair of hatches faced each other at the end of this passageway. Both were sealed, but only the left one had a ship docked at its other end. Ryke opened that hatch as lights flashed, illuminating the passageway with red.

Anguissa leaped down the shaft, hoping she wasn't insane to be trusting an *umbro*

She slid down the flume toward what had to be a small Starpod and looked back to see Ryke tapping at the console again.

Then he was spiraling toward her. They tumbled into the Starpod, one after the other. The temperature was even colder and Anguissa knew without looking at a display that the cold infinity of space was all around them. The Starpod would be attached to the underside of the larger freighter, tucked into a docking dimple, kept close for short forays.

She hoped there was a refuge close enough. Starpods didn't have much range.

Ryke locked the hatch behind them. The vessel was much larger than the Starpods Anguissa had used in the past and she was surprised by the amount of space. Ryke tapped the control console to life and entered a series of coordinates. A horn was blaring on the Armada Seven, its sound and vibration inescapable.

"They'll lock the mooring mechanism and secure us here," she noted, wondering how Ryke had overlooked that detail.

"They already have." Ryke sat back, the image of composure, and held up his hand, fingers splayed.

Five.

"Counting down. Strap in, Princess. It's going to be a bit rough."

Something flashed on the console, but Anguissa didn't recognize the language used on the instruments. She took the co-pilot seat, disliking that she was subordinate to anyone else—even the Carrier of the Seed.

Four. The scent of the Seed filled her senses, promising a satisfaction and pleasure beyond anything she'd ever known. Surely it would be worth it?

Why exactly *had* Ryke saved her? It was hard to believe he had any weaknesses at all. He was an *umbro*, after all. Had he chosen her as his next victim?

If so, what could she do to foil him? There wasn't enough room in the Starpod for her to shift shape.

Three. How long had he been preparing this escape?

Where would it end?

Would it even work?

Two. "I want the Archangel and I want it now!" Hellemut roared, her voice coming through the comm.

Anguissa gasped. "She's dead!"

"Not nearly," Ryke said grimly.

One. There was a blast from the Armada Seven. The Starpod was released from its mooring in the same moment, and so vehemently that it was flung away from the larger ship. It fell freely for long moments, then the engines fired and the Starpod accelerated away from the Armada Seven, its trajectory and speed apparently preprogrammed by Ryke.

There was another explosion, one that only hurried them on their path. Anguissa surveyed the display and tapped at the instruments, guessing how to get a view of the freighter behind them. It only took her a moment, leading her to the conclusion that the controls were similar to what she knew, despite the unfamiliar language. She stared at the display as the hold of the Armada Seven exploded into shards. The ruined remainder of the ship began to fold in on itself, and many of its lights went dark.

She shivered, not wanting to imagine the deaths of those on board.

At least those who weren't cyborgs.

She thought of Ryke tapping at consoles as they fled. He must have planted explosives in advance.

Which meant he'd been planning this escape for a while.

"I think they'll be too busy to follow us anytime soon," Ryke said with a satisfied smile.

"You've been planning this."

"No one escapes the Gloria Furore by accident. It's something I wanted to get right the first time." His manner was grim, his gaze evasive. Anguissa had the definite sense he was hiding something from her.

More than his predatory nature?

Could she claim the Seed, even if he wasn't her HeartKeeper?

"How could that have been Hellemut?"

"She has doppelgangers and they're better copies all the time."

"How many?"

"I don't know." Ryke considered this and Anguissa trusted his reaction. "I'm thinking that you took out one, but a pretty good one. The distinctions are becoming increasingly small."

"She won't be able to follow us."

"Your trashing of the deck does have some upside, Snake-Eyes." Ryke frowned at the console. "Ready to jump?"

"A Starpod can't jump," she said impatiently. "The fuselage isn't sufficiently strong and the engine..."

Anguissa fell silent because Ryke gave her a look. His eyes were twinkling and Anguissa was certain she'd never met a more alluring man. When she let the Seed guide her thinking, she couldn't find a thing wrong with him. When she used her intelligence, she knew she should be afraid of what he could do to her.

Danger *was* the spice of life, though. Anguissa leaned closer and inhaled the scent of the Seed, wanting...

"You're not the only one who doesn't follow the rules, Fire Breath," he said, recalling her to their conversation.

"Whose Starpod did we steal?"

"Captain Hellemut's personal vessel, which has had a number of very useful augmentations."

"You planned for everything."

"Not you, Snake-Eyes. I didn't plan for you."

Anguissa couldn't read his tone, which only increased her fascination with her unexpected companion. "And yet, here I am. I don't believe in coincidence, Ryke."

"Me neither." Their gazes met and held for a potent moment and Anguissa couldn't wait to get him to herself.

Naked.

"I've never had an *umbro* before," she breathed.

"And I've never had a dragon shifter."

"Why do you think our kinds find each other repellant?"

His eyes glimmered with a heat that echoed Anguissa's own. "I have no idea."

"How long is this jump?"

"Other commitments?"

Anguissa smiled. "Just paying for my passage in pleasure." She ran a fingertip up his arm and felt her toes curl with desire. Her voice turned husky. "Which can't start soon enough, to my thinking."

Ryke inhaled sharply and tore his gaze from hers. The coordinates were programmed and unfamiliar. Anguissa felt unfamiliar trepidation, but there was no time to protest.

"Prepare to jump," he said under his breath and tapped the console to commence the jump.

Anguissa's last coherent thought was a troubling one. Was it possible to fake the scent of the Seed?

Ryke dreamed.

It was the thing he hated most about jumping. He revisited all the nightmares of his past, which meant he always came out of a jump exhausted and dispirited.

This jump was no different.

He was in the small Starpod with Ryko Primus and Bakiel again. He had the warning of the freighter coming out of a jump in an unauthorized position. That wormhole had been sealed for as long as he remembered, deemed unsafe thanks to a sudden influx of astral dust. The freighter came out of the jump at alarming proximity and Ryke recharted his course so he wouldn't collide with it.

The freighter apparently recharted its course, because collision was still imminent.

"It's fine," he told his son, hoping to reassure his fears. Ryko Primus gave him a pitying glance, old enough to not be easily pacified.

"I don't think so."

The console was flashing, a warning was sounding, and Ryke was recalculating trajectories as quickly as he could. It didn't matter what he did. No matter how he changed course, the freighter loomed larger and larger on his display.

When he saw its hold open, gaping wide in the freighter's side, he knew who he confronted.

The Gloria Furore was on another slave raid.

And by being in the wrong place at the wrong time, he'd become their target.

There were no other vessels in the vicinity. There was no one to come to his aid. He was at exactly the worst point in his journey for trouble, equidistant from departing point and destination. He tried to out-distance the freighter, but knew he'd eventually lose.

The Starpod was running out of fuel. Because of the embargo, he'd been allotted enough for his planned journey and only five per cent more. It wasn't enough. The engine fell silent and Ryke's heart rose to his throat. He stared unblinking as the view of the freighter filled his display, the gaping maw of its hold obliterating everything else.

There was darkness inside the hold.

And danger.

He knew he would have the choice of whether to willingly dock his vessel inside the hold or remain unmoored. It was one of the notorious space pirates' favorite games. He could wait for the oxygen supply in his Starpod to run out and die in his vessel in their hold, or he could moor, breathe, and potentially regret every moment of his life that followed. They didn't really care. They'd sell whatever was left, either way.

"Dad?" Ryko Primus whispered, his voice rising in fear so that he sounded much younger.

"It's the Gloria Furore," Ryke supplied, his heart heavy. His son nodded even as he stared at the display in horror. "Don't worry. Your grandfather will pay your ransom. It should be quick." He nodded at Bakiel. "And your ransom will be paid, as well. *Custos* are always defended." He didn't note that this was because they were of use only to *umbros*.

"But what about you?" his son asked.

"I'll be fine, too," Ryke said, but there was no conviction in his words. He'd been publically disgraced. He'd lost all his honors. He'd abducted his son. No one paid the ransom for an outlaw.

He avoided Bakiel's gaze, knowing that his *custo* had guessed the truth as well. Ryke was going to die, slowly and painfully.

As the hold closed around the Starpod and a chill filled the small cabin, Ryke hoped he could ensure the survival of his son and *custo* first.

Anguissa opened her eyes slowly, recalling all too well that galactic workplace standards advised against jumping more than once a month in any organism's familiar time frame. She sometimes thought she had no familiar time frame anymore, not after so many years of space travel, but after three jumps in comparatively rapid succession, she knew otherwise.

She'd jumped home to Incendium. She'd left Incendium with Thalina and her robot and jumped back to the quadrant with the Armada Seven. And now she'd jumped from the vicinity of the Armada Seven to someplace else.

She hurt in places she'd forgotten she had.

She supposed it was better than the death that would have befallen her if Hellemut had caught her again, but she wasn't entirely sure.

Anguissa found water in the console and drank, knowing it was the only cure for her woes. Ryke was still apparently unconscious, though Anguissa didn't know whether to believe in appearances. Maybe he was just pretending. He certainly didn't look vulnerable.

Why *had* he saved her? She didn't know nearly enough about *umbros* and what she did know wasn't good. She stroked the film computer attached to her inner arm, but it was unresponsive. Those energy beams had probably affected its power supply, which meant that she had no ability to research or translate until it was repaired.

It was a kind of isolation that Anguissa didn't like.

She took a deep breath and found the scent of the Seed invigorating. Could she just seduce Ryke and abandon him?

It was a tempting possibility, although she thought she might always wonder about his mysteries. Anguissa frowned. He was the Carrier of the Seed, no more and no less. She *needed* to seduce him. There was no promise of a love affair or a permanent relationship. She didn't need a HeartKeeper. She just needed to satisfy her destiny and claim the Seed.

They had no fondness for each other's kinds, which probably made the whole transaction simpler. She could claim the Seed and they could part ways forever.

Where were they, anyway?

With one or two false starts, Anguissa opened the display to survey their vicinity. The Starpod was on a trajectory toward a small planet that glowed yellow in the light of its system's sun. That star had to be behind them, given the light and shadow. The planet appeared to have many, many small moons. Too many. Moons that shone in the light of the sun.

They even seemed to glitter.

Anguissa magnified the display and leaned closer, surprised to discover that they weren't moons at all.

They were ships.

Star vessels of all shapes and sizes orbited the planet. Were they occupied? Why were they here?

"Storage," Ryke said, his voice sounding as rough as she felt. Anguissa was surprised that he seemed to guess her thoughts. She glanced over to see him rub his face, then shove a hand through his hair before reaching for the controls. He had a deft touch, even though he had to be at less than his best. She found herself watching his hands and imagining them on her skin. She licked her lips, simmering, then shook her head.

The Seed was too distracting.

The sooner she had him, the better.

"The Gloria Furore keep part of their inventory of

pirated vessels here," he said. "It's a great place to shop."

"Shop?"

Again, she caught a flash of a smile, and one more time, she thought it was too brief a glimpse.

"Borrow," he ceded. "Seems only fair since they took my Starpod."

"Is it here?"

"No. Too small for their purposes. They sold it."

He was impassive and she wondered if he really felt so little, or if he felt so much that he was hiding his reaction. He had to have learned to disguise his feelings in the service of Captain Hellemut.

Assuming that he wasn't still in her service.

"You're going to steal from the Gloria Furore." Anguissa let her skepticism of that plan show in her voice.

"We already have, Snake-Eyes."

Anguissa gave him a look. "You should call me Captain Anguissa."

"You might not have noticed, but you aren't in command of a ship anymore."

"Princess Anguissa then."

"No princesses for me."

"Then call me Anguissa."

Ryke shook his head. "No way. Too personal."

That was an interesting and unexpected admission. Anguissa decided to think about that before she pursued it. "I'm sure their inventory isn't undefended..." She had time to say before the first satellites blossomed like silver sunflowers. They began to pivot toward the Starpod, so clearly targeting the vessel that Anguissa sat up a little straighter.

"We're a small target," Ryke said, as if to reassure her.

Anguissa knew better. "It's a big Starpod. Quite a nice target, really."

"One tiny fraction of misalignment and, given the

distance, the laser will miss."

"I find it hard to believe that the defense satellites of the Gloria Furore make even tiny fractional misalignments."

"Probably not. But that just means I have to be faster," Ryke mused. His fingers were dancing over the console as he programmed the nav system.

"Faster than a defense satellite programmed by the Gloria Furore? They aren't known for their poor response times."

He grinned. "Neither am I."

"It must be terrible for you to go through life with such a lack of confidence."

Ryke actually chuckled. He nodded to the far right. "We're going over there, to that freighter..."

"No," Anguissa protested. "Take the Mongossian Star Fighter. It's an older model but still has good performance..."

"But the freighter will remember me."

"*Remember* you?"

He slanted her a quick look, his eyes gleaming. "Nobody forgets me, Snake-Eyes."

Anguissa snorted. "In my experience, males of all species believe that and the vast majority of them are wrong."

"Not me, though. You'll see."

"Do you leave anyone alive to remember you?" Anguissa had to ask. "*Umbros* aren't known for letting hosts survive, much less with leaving them happy memories of shared time together." She couldn't hide her disgust of his predatory nature.

Ryke appeared to be amused. "Are you afraid of me?"

"No, but I'm wondering if I should be."

"The feeling, I assure you, is mutual." It was a strange thing to have in common, and stranger still that Anguissa found even that to be reassuring.

He gave her a sharp look, one that made her wonder whether she'd even know if he slipped into her mind.

Had he done it already?

Anguissa recoiled as he held up a finger. One of the satellites flashed red in its middle and Ryke immediately launched the nav system.

The Starpod shot fast to the right, then up, down and to the left. It spun, it zigged, it jigged and it jagged, it wobbled and it skipped until Anguissa was sure she'd lose whatever was left in her stomach. She saw the red flash of the lasers, then the Starpod ducked behind the Mongossian Star Fighter and stopped there.

"Oh no," she whispered, because she had a fondness for the vessels. Light flashed and the Star Fighter imploded. The Starpod zipped toward the freighter Ryke had pointed out and he opened the hailing frequency.

"Surely, there's no one aboard," she said beneath her breath, thinking of his comment that the ship would remember him.

A heartbeat later, a window opened on their display, showing the deck of an old freighter. A vintage android was in the captain's post, two burning red lights where a human would have eyes. "Who hails the Magnetawan?" it asked in a mechanical voice, using the universal language.

I hate robots, she mouthed, thinking it more prudent than saying the words aloud.

Ryke lifted a brow but otherwise ignored her.

So did the robot.

"Lieutenant Ryke of the Gloria Furore," Ryke said.

Anguissa blinked. Ryke had said he wasn't one of the Gloria Furore. He'd said he was slave labor. Had he lied to her, or was he lying to the robot?

She knew which answer she liked better.

"Welcome, Lieutenant," the android replied. "All is in readiness for your return. Please use bay 7C, as planned."

"I will, Piper Twelve. Please prepare to jump after we

board."

"Of course, Lieutenant," the android Piper Twelve replied. "We merely await your arrival on deck."

The hold of the Magnetawan opened slowly as the Starpod rounded the enormous vessel. Ryke accelerated so that the Starpod just zipped inside as a blaze of laser shot past them. He really was an exceptional pilot. The hold doors closed behind them, the Starpod already locked on a tractor beam to the mooring gate. There were no other vessels in the hold, which was smaller than Anguissa might have expected.

"What exactly did you do on Centurios?"

"We're all warriors."

"But you have specialties, I'm sure."

"Code," Ryke admitted easily. "My area of expertise was viruses that infect the host without leaving any sign of their presence."

Anguissa's heart chilled at this confession. Was he the one who had brought her back to the Armada Seven? If so, there could be more danger to her than she'd realized.

He spared her a wry smile that made her heart leap. "Strangely enough, I forgot to mention that to the Gloria Furore."

"When they captured you."

"Just another recruitment raid," he admitted, the corners of his mouth turning down.

"How long ago?"

"I count six years, but I'm not sure I remember all of it. It might have been longer." Ryke lifted his gaze to hers for a fleeting instant and Anguissa guessed it hadn't been an easy captivity.

"At least they didn't sell you," she said, wanting to see that rakish smile again.

"It might have been kinder if they had," he muttered. "But then, there aren't many buyers for my kind."

"*Umbros?*"

"Outlaws." He winked, probably knowing he looked disreputable, dangerous and unreliable. Her heart skipped, even as she wondered whether he was teasing her or if it was true.

"What does the Magnetawan carry?"

"Contraband, usually, but it's empty now," he said, clearly having no issues with its former trade. "It's a good thing they cleaned it out, because it'll jump farther that way. We need all the distance we can get."

It seemed unlikely to Anguissa that they'd get much distance at all with such a monstrous ship. A lot of the wormholes wouldn't have the capacity for it, and judging by its outward appearance, the stress of the jump might make some of it collapse. Ryke was out of his seat before the docking was completed, waiting at the door for the locks to engage. His confidence was unnerving.

At least he was going first.

If the reception was hostile, he'd be the one to take the hit.

One less *umbro* would make the universe a better place.

Her only regret was that she hadn't already claimed the Seed.

"Why did you save me?" she asked as the lock was engaging.

He glanced back at her. "Who says I did?"

"Not me," she admitted.

He glanced down, surprised, then leaned on the frame. "Then why did you run with me?"

"Going with you seemed like a better bet than staying on the Armada Seven. I could be completely wrong, though."

"Inclined to make mistakes, Snake-Eyes?"

"Not me. I never make mistakes."

He leaned closer, his eyes gleaming. "Nav system incinerated," he reminded her. "Which left you with no escape."

"Maybe I was counting on you."

"Bad idea. We're not known for being merciful."

"Soul-snatchers," she said.

"You should be so lucky if that's all you lose to an *umbro*."

"Why didn't you take one of them?"

His lips tightened to a grim line. "Because they wanted me to. They wanted to use me as a weapon and I refused to be used. I pretended I couldn't slip at all."

"And now?"

He smiled, looking wicked, unpredictable and delicious. "Now I have nothing left to lose. Sure you don't make mistakes?"

The Seed might have landed her in serious trouble, but she still couldn't silence its call. She reached out and touched his shoulder, feeling his strength, and nearly purred with desire.

There wasn't time for that, so Anguissa changed the subject. "How did the Magnetawan remember you?"

"I parked it here. And before I returned to the Armada Seven, I slipped a little worm into its master system, something no one would detect until I needed it."

"Just like the worm slipped into the nav system of the Archangel, the one no one detected until it brought me back to the Armada Seven."

Ryke's vivid green gaze locked with hers. "Just like."

"Did you create it?"

He grimaced. "I told you. I never admitted my skills with code to the Gloria Furore. They trusted me only as a pilot."

"Did you install the worm in the Archangel?"

"No."

"Why should I believe you?"

"Because it's true." The door slid open, revealing a small chamber with an airlock on the other side.

"And where are we going, Ryke?"

"Home. Of course." He shrugged. "At least I am. I don't know where you're going."

"For the moment, I'm going with you," she said, following him out of the Starpod.

He gave her a cocky grin. "Because you want to repay me for helping you escape?"

"Because you have something I want and once I have it, we can go our separate ways." The more she learned, the more Anguissa was determined to keep her relationship with Ryke as short as possible.

"And what would that be?" he asked as they stepped through the airlock into the next sealed chamber. "Information? Directions? Fabulous sex?" It was clear he said the last as a joke, but Anguissa smiled at him.

"Lots of sex." She backed him into the wall and caught his face in her hands, staring into his eyes. "You could consider it your reward. I know I will." She didn't give him a chance to answer, but kissed him fiercely to silence.

It took less than a nanosecond for Ryke to wrap his arms around her and draw her tightly against him, then angle his head and deepen their kiss.

The scent of the Seed surged to new power and Anguissa considered the merit of having him right then and there.

Anguissa's first kiss had been only a taste of her fire. This second one made Ryke sizzle right to his toes. He'd been celibate too long by any accounting, but Anguissa's kiss more than made up for whatever he'd been missing. The strange thing was that he liked that she wasn't shy and that she demanded exactly what she wanted. He liked that she seized him and kissed him and slid her tongue between his teeth. He preferred passive and compliant women—that's what he knew best—but there was something electric about Anguissa's bold demands. Those fabulous breasts were crushed against him and he grabbed her perfect butt, lifting her against him.

He wanted more.

He wanted all she had to give.

He'd never wanted a woman the way he wanted Anguissa. Right here and right now. Fast and hard. And then again. It had to be the novelty or sheer desperation, but for the moment, Ryke didn't care. He wanted to strip her out of her suit and claim her over and over and over again, to frack with the Gloria Furore and Captain Hellemut and anyone else stupid enough to get in the way.

But he hadn't come this far to get captured again before his escape was complete.

In fact, her effect upon him was proof that all the old stories were true. An abomination like a dragon shifter could mess up his priorities, change his thinking, persuade him to make a foolish choice.

If he stayed with Anguissa, he could be a dead man.

Strange how being with her made him feel so alive, as if he'd awakened for the first time. Was that part of her power?

He broke their kiss with an effort, liking the heat in her eyes. Those flames were back, the ones that reminded him of her truth, and he found it exciting that she was so dangerous. Her hair looked like snakes again and he smiled that they were writhing.

Just the way he felt like writhing with her.

Once couldn't hurt.

And then he'd know what it was like.

"Resistance is futile, Ryke," she purred, her passion making him want to forget the Gloria Furore even more than he did.

"Let's get out of here first," he said, then led her to the next airlock. He was almost running in his haste to get to the deck, but it was a desire to get the jump behind them so he could seduce Anguissa that was making him run, not the need to escape.

They reached the deck and strapped down simultaneously. She took a long swig of water as Piper Twelve presented the nav system to Ryke for him to approve the coordinates of their pre-set destination. It was three short jumps home, and he took the opportunity to pre-program the intermediary cruises in case he felt too lousy to fly. He started the rejuvenation for Bakiel, who was in stasis in the hold.

By the time they got to Centurios, he'd feel like something that should be scraped off the bottom of his boot. Anguissa would probably feel worse, given that she'd done at least another jump before him.

But it was the only way out.

At least Bakiel would be awake.

A laser collided with the hull and shook the freighter, as if to remind him to hurry. Ryke looked at Anguissa, she nodded, and they jumped.

Resistance is futile.

Anguissa's words summoned Ryke's nightmare. He dreamed of his days and nights on the moon of Formican, where he had been tested by the Gloria Furore for his endurance. He'd been right about the ransom— no one on Centurios had paid for him—and the pirates hadn't managed to sell a reputed *umbro* to anyone else without proof of his abilities. He refused to slip and show his skills, because of that old vow to be different. Instead, they chose to use him as a test, to discover the limits of his endurance to refine their torture protocol.

It was supposed to break him.

Instead, the torture hardened everything within Ryke, forging his anger into a determination to survive that would never abandon him. The legacy of Formican's moon was Ryke's resolve to never surrender, to never yield, and to never ever reveal his depth of his hatred for his captors. Everything became black and white to him, simple and linear, with the need to survive trumping every other objective.

It had only taken three baths in fire ants to convince him to pretend to crumble. He'd never forget the pain of millions of pincers biting and gnawing through his flesh. He'd never forget the weeks of agony as the wounds healed. He'd certainly never forget the unguents that were applied to his skin to make the torment last longer.

It had been the worst period of his life.

It had taught him to lie, to hate, and to plan for vengeance. It had forged him into a different man, one fueled by fury.

He'd had to convince the interrogator to believe him, but do it without slipping. It hadn't been easy, but Ryke had succeeded.

In his nightmare, though, he relived the failure, not the triumph. He was immersed to the neck in fire ants one more time. They were biting and chewing at his flesh, thousands and thousands of them. Every increment of his body hurt or burned or was in anguish. He struggled, unable to break away from them. Of course not. The baths were vats filled with fire ants, vats into which prisoners like Ryke were lowered slowly, left, then raised to relief.

And lowered again.

It was as excruciating as he remembered but he was surprised to realize this time that his hands weren't bound. He swatted at his shoulder when he was bitten, and his hand was immediately bitten, too.

It wasn't a dream.

The bite was too big.

Ryke opened his eyes to find the jump completed, the freighter drifting close to a red sun, and the snakes of

Anguissa's hair snapping at him. She was still unconscious from the jump, but her snakes were wide awake. They twisted in agitation, their eyes shining bright yellow, and he assumed he had been wrong about them revealing her innermost thoughts.

He felt rather than heard someone step onto the deck. Everything within him quickened with the certainty that they were in peril.

Who else was on board?

Ryke reached for the weapon he'd taken from Anguissa on the Armada Seven and spun to his feet, firing at the portal. Anguissa had already leaped into action. Apparently, she hadn't been asleep. She vaulted over the deck, shifting to her dragon form in the blink of an eye, and fried the android at the portal.

There was no sign of Piper Twelve.

Ryke struggled to follow her, shaking off the shards of his nightmare. Anguissa seemed to show no ill effects from the jump. She reached one claw through the doorway. She hauled half a dozen struggling androids back through the opening and crushed them between her talons. There was weapon fire on the other side of the door and she glanced to Ryke.

She had to shift to go through the door or risk destroying the air lock.

He nodded, moving to cover her. She flung the shattered androids through the door and Ryke stepped forward to fire, intending to create chaos on the other side.

"Thirty," he muttered, glad it wasn't more but wishing there might have been fewer of them. Anguissa darted through the door and shifted to her dragon form on the other side. He wondered if there were any limitations to how often she could do that. The android soldiers fired their weapons and charged, even as Anguissa loosed a stream of dragon fire on them.

Ryke could feel the heat of their metal shells and smelled circuits burning. They continued, though, unable to stop themselves from following the command, and he fired into their midst. He blinded some and shot off the limbs of others. Anguissa shredded the ones foolish enough to get close to her and smashed others against the walls. She crushed them underfoot, casting Ryke weapons as she destroyed the androids carrying them.

The battle was over with ridiculous speed. Ryke sighed and pushed a hand through his hair as he surveyed the smoking debris.

"Don't tell me," he said. "You hate robots."

Instead of answering him, Anguissa's eyes flashed with fire. She leaped toward him and smashed an android into the wall behind him. Ryke hadn't even heard that one approaching.

It slid down the wall, not quite finished, and appealed to him for mercy with one outstretched mechanical hand. The gesture reminded him too clearly of Hellemut's last appeal. He raised his weapon and fired into its eyes, extinguishing one after the other.

Anguissa would have ripped out its circuitry, but he held up a hand to stop her. She waited, watching as Ryke typed a message into the console on the android's chest.

"Mission accomplished," it said in a broken voice, then Ryke nodded.

Anguissa shredded the android, smashing its remains on the floor. He admired her thoroughness and her strength.

She shifted shape and stood beside him, her breath coming quickly. "Mission accomplished?" she echoed, and glanced up at him.

"Someone gave the command to attack. It stood to reason that it might still be in contact with that someone."

"It would have been if you had programmed it."

"Exactly. It was important they didn't have time to ask *whose* mission was accomplished."

Her smile was fleeting. "I hope there's a crusher on the trash disposal," she said, surveying the damage. "And a means of jettisoning it all. I'm not sleeping with any of these bits still on the ship."

What had happened to give her such a distrust of robots?

"When did you start planning to sleep?" he asked and she laughed.

"Afterward, you'll need to."

Ryke thought they both would. He intended to make sure of it.

"There's a crusher right down here," he said and began to sweep the chunks toward the disposal.

Anguissa helped. "How much do you know about this ship anyway?"

"I thought as much as I needed to."

"Which means you didn't know about *them*."

"They weren't here the last time I was."

"Sounds like you really might be unforgettable, Ryke, and that you pissed someone off." Anguissa almost smiled. "Does this count as a mistake?"

Ryke grinned despite himself. "Maybe we're even, Snake-Eyes."

"What happens next?"

"Half a day cruise until the next jump."

Anguissa groaned. "How many more?"

"Just two more short ones until home. Look on the bright side. We can scatter this debris in the wormhole and make it tougher for anyone following us."

"That *is* a bright side." She swept with greater purpose, clearly unafraid of hard work. He stole glances at her as they worked together, admiring more than her inviting curves. She was practical and tough, as well as sexy.

He wished she could have simply been a woman, instead of a dragon shifter. If women had been like this on Centurios, Ryke wouldn't have been so determined to remain unattached.

But Anguissa was a dragon shifter, and he needed to keep that in mind. Even though he had a feeling Anguissa was trouble and then some, he was looking forward to her making it worth his while to rescue her. What would she be like as a lover? He couldn't imagine her surrendering to anyone over anything, but he'd never been with a demanding lover either.

The women of Centurios, including the mother of his son, simply let intimacy happen to them. They didn't participate. They didn't reciprocate. The princesses of Centurios were the highest caste of passive women, kept and pampered so they could service the most powerful men in the realm—or the sons of those men. They knew their place. They were ornamental. Useful for the procreation of children. Interchangeable and forgettable. Mostly silent.

Ryke couldn't remember a woman who made choices, let alone demands. He didn't know any who had opinions or spoke up, or explained what they wanted. He'd never known one who could have fired a weapon or fought, much less won a battle or defended his back.

Ryke had a feeling sex was going to be really different with Anguissa.

Maybe he was going to have to tame her.

He couldn't wait to find out.

Chapter Three

"What kind of princess are you, anyway?" Ryke asked and Anguissa flashed him a look.

"A runaway one." Her smile was rueful. "I'm no diplomat. Court life wasn't for me."

Did that make them two of a kind? "But shipping contraband was?"

She seemed to hold back a laugh. Her eyes were twinkling and it was easy to forget that she was a dragon shifter who could annihilate anything or anyone she chose. "They sent me to law school, which was a big mistake."

Ryke found himself smiling, even as he tried to remember the truth of her nature and its effect upon his kind. "You know enough to keep yourself out of trouble."

Anguissa nodded. "You see, it's not technically contraband most of the time. Where I make acquisitions, my purchases are perfectly legal. It's the delivery of them in places where they aren't legal that puts me outside the law. I never linger, so the vast majority of the time, I'm not in violation of local or intergalactic law."

"What about on Incendium?"

"I like to think my father would be merciful, but that might be optimistic."

Ryke snorted.

"It sounds like you share my skepticism."

"In my experience, fathers can't be relied upon to be merciful, not when the alternative is upholding the law."

She leaned on her sweeper and considered him. "'Duty first and above all else' could be my father's motto, Soul-Stealer."

"Mine, too, Fire-Starter."

Instead of being insulted or offended, Anguissa laughed and resumed sweeping. "I've never tested him on it because he can be pretty tough. I usually arrive in home port with an empty hold."

"Usually?"

"Not this last time. I have to wonder what he made of that haul." She shrugged but he sensed that she was troubled by something. What had she been carrying? For the first time in a very long time, Ryke was tempted to slip into someone else's mind—but he didn't want to risk losing the company of this unexpectedly interesting princess. "It's probably all been incinerated by now. Too bad. I hadn't had a good look at it all."

"You bought a haul without looking? That doesn't seem very sensible."

"Not sensible at all. It was impulsive." She was unapologetic. As a man who planned every detail and always had, Ryke was fascinated and appalled. "I was curious."

"You know what they say about curiosity."

Anguissa laughed easily. "And it's true! It was an auction. Big lots, no investigation, being sold in a hurry. Just the circumstances made me think the goods might be interesting to someone somewhere."

"But you never looked?"

"There was no chance."

"Even after you bought?"

"The auction was raided just as we were loading it all." She averted her gaze, even turning her back on him, and Ryke wondered if this was all true. "We didn't wait to see which authority it was, but got out of there fast. We had to jump long to have a chance, so I went straight for Incendium. You know how it is in a long jump. If you're lucky, you miss most of it and wake up feeling like junk. If you're unlucky, it feels as if time has stretched just to make you pay for your sins."

Ryke nodded agreement. He thought about mentioning the nightmares but decided against it. That was probably the price of his personal sins.

"We'd only just docked when my sister asked for my help." Anguissa paused and looked up, her shock clear. "Which means Thalina is sitting on that stash. Frack, I hope it's not as dangerous as I suspected it might be."

"Your sister's not a fighter?"

"My sister is too precise for battle. No broad-stroke solutions for Thalina. She has to get all the details exactly right, no matter how long it takes."

"Warfare wouldn't be her strength."

"Not fighting in the thick of it. She'd have to calculate every blow and look for the ideal strike. She'd be a good strategist, though, planning the battle ahead of time."

"When she had time to consider all the possibilities."

"Exactly. She makes amazing automatons. The only thing we have in common besides lineage is that we both do something that our father disapproves of."

Ryke snorted.

"You have sisters or brothers, Ryke?"

"No. My father said he only needed one son."

"And your mother?"

Ryke blinked. "I doubt anyone asked her."

Anguissa's eyes narrowed. "Why am I thinking that I wouldn't love Centurios?"

"You wouldn't see its best side. Once your nature was known, it would be the arena for you."

"The arena?"

"Blood sport for entertainment. Abominations have to be destroyed, so there might as well be entertainment."

Anguissa grimaced. "Always blood," she mused, then turned away from him again. Ryke felt the change in her mood.

"What are you thinking about?"

"I'm remembering the wreckage left by an *umbro* that I saw in a space bar once," she said quietly, then eyed him with distrust. "Why did you have to be one of them?"

"I was born one," Ryke replied, well accustomed to her reaction. On Centurios, his kind were revered, but elsewhere, they were feared—and really, the reverence on Centurios was probably rooted in fear. "But I can choose how and when I use my powers." He impaled her with a glance. "Why did you have to be a dragon shifter?"

She smiled. "I was born one, but I can choose how and when I use my powers." She leaned on her sweeper. "Let's make a deal, Ryke."

"What kind of deal?"

"I won't incinerate you and leave toasted shards of you in a corner, and you won't invade my mind and leave me to bleed to death."

Ryke wouldn't have done that anyway, but he appreciated that she'd reciprocate. "Deal," he said and offered his hand.

Anguissa smiled and slid her hand into his, her touch making him aware of how smooth her skin was. She gripped his hand, almost as strong as him, and closed the distance between them so that her breasts bumped against his chest. He could smell her skin and her arousal, the combination sending fire through his veins. "A handshake, Ryke?" she asked, a teasing tone in her voice.

"It's just a start," he acknowledged, then bent and kiss her.

"A ruse, maybe?" she murmured, her lips almost

against his.

"An invitation," he clarified, then kissed her again. He meant the embrace to be quick, but Anguissa opened her mouth and slid her tongue across his lips. Her move felt wanton and inviting, and rare in his experience for that.

Ryke dropped his sweeper and caught Anguissa in his arms, backing her into the wall as he deepened his kiss. She made a little growl of satisfaction that drove him wild, then seized a fistful of his hair when she tipped her head back and surrendered to him. He feasted upon her, wanting her more than he'd wanted anyone in a long time, yet amazed that her reaction excited him so much. She hooked her leg around his and rubbed herself against his erection, making Ryke think of taking her immediately.

"Here," she breathed when he broke their kiss. He ran kisses along her jaw to her ear, liking how she shivered. "Now," she demanded and he realized that she would happily take control of their union.

He stepped back with an effort, locking his hands around her waist and putting space between them. "You're demanding, Snake-Eyes," he murmured, liking the heat in her eyes.

"I know what I want," she breathed. "I have no issues explaining."

"I know what I want, too."

"Tell me, Ryke."

"I like women to be submissive, to come when they're called, to do what they're told, to wait for me and my pleasure."

Anguissa laughed, then ran a hand down his chest and over his erection. "You could have fooled me, Ryke. I'm none of those things but you seem to like me just fine." Her eyes sparkled. "Maybe variety is the spice of life."

"Maybe you need a lesson," he growled and her smile

turned seductive.

"Are you volunteering for the job?" She was teasing him with her fingertips, her gaze knowing. Ryke gave serious consideration to tossing her over his shoulder, carrying her to some dark corner, and having his fill of her.

He turned away, knowing that she was manipulating him too easily. He was the *umbro*! He was the one who decided who should serve him and when. "Sounds to me like you're a bit spoiled, Princess," he muttered and picked up his sweeper again.

She didn't argue with him, but he felt her watching him.

What was she thinking?

He stifled his natural inclination to slip, reminding himself of his vow. Strange how she tempted him to do what he'd sworn not to do again.

But then, Ryke wasn't really surprised. Anguissa had a talent for provoking him.

They shoved the last of the debris into the waste collector and Ryke activated the crusher. Only when it was finished the cycle did Anguissa lean back against the wall and appear to relax. "Did you know that I hate robots?" she asked lightly.

"I believe you mentioned it."

Anguissa frowned. "Here's the thing. My sister says her Carrier of the Seed is a cyborg. He might even be her HeartKeeper, which is a terrifying prospect indeed."

"Should that make sense to me?"

She spared him a glance then straightened, as if she'd said too much. "No. And it doesn't matter, anyway." She pushed away from the wall and he sensed her putting barriers between them again.

Ryke reminded himself that he didn't want to get to know her, much less to have any feelings for her. Even though she was intriguing. She challenged his every expectation of princesses and of women, and continually surprised him.

Maybe that was a dragon shifter trait.

Either way, he couldn't resist asking one question.

"You mentioned the Seed before," he reminded her, sensing that it was important but not knowing why.

Anguissa inhaled again, that familiar lustful gleam lighting her eyes. The reaction of Ryke's body to the sight was becoming familiar, too. "Mmm, yes, the Seed. It's what got me into this mess." She tipped her head back and met his gaze. Her smile was sultry and inviting.

Had he ever met a more enticing woman?

"Too bad you don't like kissing, Ryke."

"Who says I don't?"

"You stopped," she reminded him, tapping a finger on his chest. "Maybe it's dragon shifters you don't like."

"Which is only fair, since you don't like *umbros*."

"And here I thought we'd made a temporary amnesty."

"So did I. Backing out?"

"Not a chance."

Ryke fitted his hands around her waist again and lifted her against him, liking that she didn't protest at all. Anguissa's smile broadened and the heat rose between them. "I believe you offered to make it worth my while to help you escape," he reminded her.

"Have we escaped, Ryke?"

"Almost," he ceded. "There is still a chance of pursuit. There always will be."

"I like interim rewards." She flattened her hands and ran them across his chest, then slid her fingers beneath his shirt. The feel of her fingertips against his bare skin sent lust surging through Ryke.

He swallowed. "We could, alternatively, celebrate our avoidance of certain death." He felt himself smile. "I could make *that* worth your while."

Anguissa chuckled. She crushed him a little harder against the wall—which was pretty much exactly where Ryke wanted to be—and wrapped her hand around his nape to pull his head down for a kiss.

"We could," she agreed, her voice husky, then ran a hand over him. Her touch was bold and proprietary, unlike that of any woman Ryke had ever known, and he liked it just fine. "Are you a good lover, Ryke?" she breathed.

"A phenomenal one," he confessed, kissing her quickly. "Thorough." He punctuated that with another kiss. "With exceptional stamina."

"And well-endowed," she said with a firm caress.

"A champion in every way. Care to find out for yourself?"

"Absolutely." Her eyes were dancing with laughter. "I just wish there was a way to build your confidence, Ryke."

"Just surrender to me, Snake-Eyes," he growled. "And I'll show you." He captured her lips then and held her just where he wanted her to be, feasting upon her mouth and holding her captive against him.

"That could be a dealbreaker," she whispered when he gave her a chance. Those flames were glowing in her eyes again.

"How so? You don't like pleasure?"

"Of course, but surrender is out of the question. I like to be on top."

"Not a chance. That's not where a woman belongs."

Her snakes hissed as Anguissa stepped back. "Belongs?" she echoed, a warning in her tone.

"Belongs," Ryke affirmed and reached for her again. "Surrender and I'll convince you."

Anguissa moved quickly, hooking her heel behind his and tripping him. Ryke fell, surprised by her assault, and rolled to his back.

Only to find Anguissa straddling him, her satisfaction clear. "This is much better," she said and bent to kiss him.

Ryke rolled her immediately to her back, pinning her down and kissing her fiercely to stake his claim. She kissed him back, undaunted, and the fire in his veins grew to an inferno. His reaction was primal and fierce. It was all he could do to keep from claiming her right there, when she squirmed beneath him and knotted her hands in his hair, pulling him closer and demanding more.

"I'll change your mind," he said when he finally lifted his head.

Anguissa smiled and ran one hand down his chest, around his waist, then gripped his butt. "Tell me, Ryke, does this heap of junk have decent hygiene facilities?"

"Why do you think I picked it?"

"No idea. It can't have been for the decor or the company."

He bit back a smile, liking that nothing seemed to diminish her passion for life. "Let me show you, Princess."

"That's Snake-Eyes to you," she retorted, but she didn't fight him when he stood up and cast her over his shoulder, carrying her to the captain's quarters.

He'd won and he'd make sure she didn't regret it.

Anguissa was surprised to find every possible comfort installed in the captain's quarters of the ugliest freighter she'd seen in a long while. It was a comfortable refuge, decorated in a deep plum shade that she found luxurious and pleasing. Ryke had put the vessel into a slow spin that was an elegant way of providing a comfortable level of gravity. She would have thought the freighter was too ungainly for the trick, but she'd already noticed Ryke's skill at the helm.

She wondered if he needed a job, now that he'd

escaped the Gloria Furore. She could always use a good pilot.

Assuming she ever retrieved the Archangel. It made her heart clench to think she might have lost the vessel that she loved more than life itself.

So, she didn't think about it.

She thought about the Seed instead.

And the claiming of it.

Anguissa took a deep breath, letting the scent fill her lungs and feed her passion. In the small space, she was more aware of Ryke—of how tall and broad he was, of what an excellent physical specimen he was—and she thrilled at the prospect of seducing him. She deliberately forgot his nature.

The portal was sealed. The bed was soft. Ryke was clearly ready for her and she was looking forward to exploring him.

He wanted to dominate her, it was clear, and Anguissa's need for the Seed was so intense that she was considering the merit of humoring him.

On the other hand, changing things from his usual pattern might excite him even more.

It certainly would excite Anguissa. She wanted the claiming of the Seed to be a memorable mating.

Ryke secured the door, and she guessed by his expression that he liked having her captive in the space. "Does this make me your concubine?" she asked. "The captain's captive?"

Ryke's eyes glowed. "I'm thinking so."

"Then I'd better do your will," she said. "And serve your needs."

"An excellent plan."

The Seed seemed to intensify in the small space, the heady scent of it making Anguissa dizzy—and wet with desire. "What do you like, Ryke?" she asked, trying to sound subdued and probably failing.

"Skin. I like skin. Let me see you."

Anguissa faced Ryke, then tugged her shirt over her head. Her breasts bounced slightly and she saw his eyes brighten as he surveyed them. She kicked off her boots and peeled off her tights, then shook out her hair. She felt the snakes rise, echoing her own excitement as they stretched wide around her head.

He was looking at her, obviously appreciating her figure. She spun, displaying herself to him. "Will I do?" she teased and he made a growl of approval.

She supposed she should serve him. She moved closer and untucked the top of his uniform. She could see a band of tanned flesh and ran her hand across it, liking how muscled he was. She slid her hands beneath his shirt, pushing it over his head and baring his chest to her view.

Then she stopped to stare at the thousands, maybe millions, of tiny scars. She shouldn't stare, she knew it, but she couldn't help herself.

"Fire ants," she whispered, running her fingertips over the distinctive marks. They covered Ryke's skin, making him look tanned, and she was astonished by the sheer number of them.

"I don't recommend Formican's moon as a vacation destination," he said tightly.

Anguissa flicked a glance at his eyes, which were too serious. "It's not a resort. It's a penal colony."

He nodded, impassive. "Ah. That explains it, then."

Anguissa shivered, because she had heard stories of the vats of fire ants there, of the torment inflicted upon prisoners. The line of scars stopped at his throat, just under his chin, meaning that he'd been dipped up to his neck in them. Judging by the number of scars and the variation in their color, it had happened more than once. He watched her, his gaze unflinching.

"Changing your mind?" he asked, his voice a rumble.

He'd survived and she admired that. He wasn't bitter

or vengeful, which she respected even more.

"Not a chance," she admitted, letting him see her admiration. "I like a lover with stamina."

Ryke snorted.

How had torture changed him? It changed everyone in some way, Anguissa knew, because it was designed to do as much. Bond always said good torture fucked with the mind and left it damaged forever. Maybe Ryke's experience on Formican's moon was why he didn't confide very much very readily.

If so, that was a pretty small price to have paid.

He kicked off his own boots, then turned his back on her to remove the bottom of his uniform. When he turned to face her, his enthusiasm was obvious and his size impressive.

She pushed him to the sleeping couch and he caught her around the waist before he fell backward. "I'll be the captain and you'll be the captive," she whispered just before she kissed him.

"Not a chance," he said, then rolled her to her back. He braced himself above her, then cupped her breast in his other hand. He pinched the nipple enough to make her squirm, then bent to kiss it thoroughly. "Looks like there's going to be a mutiny under your command."

It clearly was important to Ryke to be in charge of their seduction. Anguissa decided to let him him take the lead the first time.

"What do you intend to do with your prisoner?" she asked, her voice catching as his tongue did wicked things to her nipple.

"It's only sensible for me to determine exactly how dragon shifter princesses differ from other women I've known."

"Sounds like a quest you're going to take seriously."

"Very seriously," he growled. "The only difference I see in your basic physiology is the snakes." She looked up to find his gaze locked upon her. "Any chance you could turn them off?"

"They're part of me," she said, curious that he might be afraid of anything at all.

"And I like how they reveal your thoughts. It's useful in battle, and even a bit hot."

"Hot?" Anguissa echoed.

"Yes. When you're standing there, eyes flashing, hair writhing, you could lead a company of warriors to their death with no trouble at all."

Anguissa smiled at the compliment, which he delivered in a matter-of-fact tone, as if it was indisputable. "Thank you."

"But right here and right now..." Ryke shook his head.

"Not so good for you?"

He grimaced. "You and robots. Me and snakes in bed."

Anguissa chuckled. "How about a blindfold? Then you wouldn't have to see them." She stole a quick kiss then whispered in his ear. "I like blindfolding my lovers."

"No," Ryke snapped and pulled away, the humor banished from his eyes.

Anguissa knew she'd found a nerve and she speculated that the Gloria Furore had blindfolded him at some point—and whatever had happened subsequently hadn't been good. She sighed with mock forbearance, hoping she could restore his playful mood.

Maybe there was a good reason he liked to be in charge.

"You really aren't going to be a very willing sex slave, are you?"

The gleam was immediately back in his eyes. "The way I remember it, you're the sex slave, Snake-Eyes."

Anguissa laughed. "I'm not good at being submissive."

"That's not a surprise, but maybe I know what you want better than you do."

"Oh, I don't think so," she purred. "But that's a challenge I can't refuse." Anguissa sat up and braided the snakes back, whispering to them to soothe them. They stilled at her command and she spared Ryke a glance. "Better?"

"Perfect," he said with satisfaction. "Just perfect."

"Then go ahead, Ryke, and finish your inventory."

"With pleasure," Ryke murmured, closing the distance between them. His hands ran over her with possessive ease, his touch making her shiver.

Making her yearn.

Anguissa parted her lips, inviting his touch. Ryke smiled just a little.

Then his mouth closed over hers with a proprietary ease that bode very, very well for the immediate future.

Ryke couldn't have imagined a more ideal partner for ending his lengthy run of enforced celibacy, even though he would never have imagined it could be so. Anguissa was beautiful and passionate, unafraid of her desires. He loved the ripe swell of her breasts and the responsiveness of her body. She was so different from his past lovers, so engaged, that he felt he could have been making love for the first time ever.

He could even forget the snakes with the right encouragement, which was exactly what Anguissa gave him.

He loved the sweet crush of her beneath him, the feel of her foot sliding up and down his calf. Her hands were locked on his shoulders, her head tipped back and her eyes closed. She was fearless and seductive, prepared to welcome whatever he gave. He broke their kiss and couldn't resist the urge to trail kisses to her ear.

"You kiss like other women," he whispered and she

shivered against him at the feel of his breath.

"Then I wasn't doing it right," she replied and he found himself smiling again.

She caught his head in her hands and gave him another kiss, an open-mouthed hungry one that made his heart pound. When she tore her mouth from his, her eyes were glittering and her lips were a little swollen.

"Maybe not quite like other women I've known," Ryke acknowledged. "Although your lips appear to be similar."

"It's all in the technique," she growled and claimed his mouth again. She tried to roll him to his back but Ryke braced himself over her, refusing to succumb. Anguissa kept kissing him and he didn't want her to stop. The sleeping couch was covered with a soft fabric, but with that against his skin and Anguissa beneath him, he was sure he was in paradise. He lifted her breast on his palm again, He ran his thumb across the nipple and she arched her back, rubbing herself against him with pleasure.

"The only thing unusual about your breast is how responsive the nipple is."

"Maybe I like you," Anguissa murmured, her eyes glowing.

"Maybe I'm good at this," he countered, catching the tight peak between finger and thumb.

Anguissa gasped. "Maybe you are," she managed to say, a wonderful tension in her voice. "Just don't stop."

Ryke grinned, then bent to take the nipple in his mouth. He kissed it, gently at first, then with increasing demands. He thought Anguissa might ask him to stop, as other lovers had done, but she clearly reveled in his touch. She writhed beneath him, digging her nails into his shoulders, then locked one leg over his hip.

He immediately smelled the sweet scent of her arousal. He slid his hand down to caress her and was pleasantly surprised to discover how wet she was. Other women might need encouragement—or even lubricants—but Anguissa wanted him and her body showed the truth. That was thrilling. It was honest. Her responsiveness was a novelty he could get used to. He touched her gently, finding the hard bead of her arousal and couldn't resist temptation.

He abandoned her nipple and kissed his way down the firm length of her to the apex of her thighs. He inhaled deeply of the scent of her, finding it incredibly exciting that she wanted him so much, then flicked his tongue against her. Anguissa emitted a little helpless cry, all the more thrilling because he couldn't imagine her helpless at all, then spread her legs wide in capitulation. Ryke accepted the silent invitation and lowered himself between her thighs to feast upon her.

She was so slick with her arousal that Ryke couldn't believe it. He teased her with his tongue, liking that he had the power to give her such pleasure. She whispered his name and gripped his shoulders as he coaxed her higher, and he gripped her more tightly when she began to twist against him. He felt her tremble deep inside and he heard her pleas become incoherent.

He drove her on, higher and harder, relentless in his determination to give her as much pleasure as possible. To teach her that his way was best. To convince her to return for more. When she was quivering, her legs locked around him, her hands gripping his hair, he stopped and she cried out with dismay.

"Together," he muttered, wiping his mouth and climbing atop her. Anguissa didn't hesitate. She wrapped her legs around his waist, pulling him deep inside the soft heat of her. He had to lean his forehead on her shoulder, awed by the wave of satisfaction he felt in burying himself inside her, and he felt himself shake with the effort of restraining himself.

Anguissa seemed to guess his thoughts, which should have warned him.

"Don't hold back," she whispered in his ear. "Take me as hard as you want, then take me again. You can't hurt me." He looked into her eyes and saw that fearlessness again, the sight better than any aphrodisiac. "I want to be claimed, Ryke. I want to be possessed. I want to be taken harder and faster than ever before." The corner of her mouth lifted as she surveyed him. "I have a feeling you might be the right man for the job."

Ryke didn't wait to be asked twice. She could have been demanding that he fulfill his own fantasy. He moved within her, loving her snug velvet heat, then thrust deep. Anguissa growled with satisfaction and gripped his shoulders, demanding more. Her nails dug into his skin and he moved deeper, liking how she rose to meet him. She caught his face in her hands and kissed him as if she would never get enough of him.

As if she might eat him alive.

Ryke was completely seduced. If she had been his captive, he was sure he'd never let her go. The very idea drove him wild. He thrust with increasing speed, wanting the moment to last forever and knowing it couldn't possibly. All the years of denial fed the force of this union. All the suppressed desire, all the sacrifices fed the overwhelming sweetness of this moment, of this interval, of this woman. She met him touch for touch, inviting him onward, demanding more, her passion redoubling his own.

He felt the tremble of her release begin like a seismic shudder deep inside her. She whispered his name and then begged incoherently for satisfaction, a sight of vulnerability in this powerful woman that destroyed Ryke completely.

He drove himself against her and she shouted, locking around him as she came. He gripped her tightly as he buried himself deeply inside her one last time and roared with the fury of his own orgasm.

He felt as if he had been dropped into the heart of the sun, to be burned to nothing and made new again.

As he rolled to his back, spent and panting, Ryke knew that he would never be the same again.

Mission accomplished.

Anguissa closed her eyes, savoring the bliss.

She and Ryke lay together, their legs tangled, the cabin filled with the scent of their shared pleasure. Anguissa felt her heart slow its pace, gradually returning to normal, but she wasn't in a hurry to move. Ryke looked as if he was sleeping, but she was pretty sure he was just hiding his thoughts from her.

Again.

Unraveling his secrets would have to be some other woman's pleasure. Anguissa felt a teeny bit of regret, but the Seed had been claimed. Her quest was complete. Their paths would part as soon as possible.

But she couldn't resist the urge to tease Ryke just a little.

She heaved a sigh. "All right," she said, as if making a great concession. "You *are* good at this. I can't argue with that."

His eyes opened just a little, making him look unpredictable. Still cocky. Still sexy. So delicious that it might be worth another round. She still could teach him the pleasures of lady on top. Anguissa ran a hand over him, halfway wishing this could be more than a biological imperative.

But that would be ridiculously complicated.

It was strange. She should be revolted by him and his nature. Her very reasonable horror of *umbros* and their dark powers should have returned, now that the Seed was satisfied. But she found Ryke just as attractive as she had before, and she wanted him again.

Maybe the Seed undermined her common sense permanently.

"I didn't expect such an easy victory," he murmured, his chest vibrating beneath her hand. "I was sure you'd want three or even four demonstrations to be sure."

"That's a tempting suggestion," she ceded, dropping her weight onto his chest and giving him a kiss. "Maybe I should just say that you're always right, that your confidence is deserved, and let you have your way with me."

He rolled his eyes as if that was unlikely and sat up with her in his lap. "I have my limitations, Snake-Eyes. Maybe it's time to explore those hygiene facilities."

Another kiss and they abandoned the couch as one, moving to the hygiene unit. "How much sex did you get while in the company of the Gloria Furore?" She had to ask.

His expression immediately closed. "None. Mercifully."

She reached out and touched the tip of his member, which was marked with the same scars as everywhere else on his body. "Fire ants even there?"

He glared at her. "I don't want to talk about it."

She stretched up to brush her lips across his. "Of course, you don't. You're nothing if not predictable, Blood-Dealer."

"What's that supposed to mean?"

"That you like having your secrets. Fine by me."

Ryke snorted, but she could see that he was pleased. His expression changed with her next words.

"Does this hulk have a good star map?"

"Why?" His suspicion was more than evident.

"Because I need to figure out where I'm going to get off. I'll look at your charted route and decide." She glanced around the cabin. "This wreck is probably old enough to have a chart room."

"It does."

"Well, that will be a novelty, at least." She shuddered elaborately. "I have to say, it's very strange to be unaware of my own coordinates, never mind your flight path."

Ryke was impassive but she could feel his disapproval. "I thought we were in this together."

"We were, but it's done." Anguissa finished cleaning herself up and tugged on her clothes. "I know you'll miss me. Maybe you'll be haunted by the memory of our time together." She smiled at the very idea and shook her head. "Don't argue, please. Just leave me with my illusions. I know I'll remember this. It'll probably be the one and only time I ever let my partner dominate me."

"How can you think anything is done?" Ryke flung out a hand and sounded more agitated than Anguissa had expected.

"Don't tell me you're going to argue for a shared future?" she scoffed. "Ryke, you're a practical man. I'm not a romantic. You're an *umbro* and I'm a dragon shifter. Our kinds hate each other. Don't feel obliged to make that argument for my sake. We're done." She watched as he shoved a hand through his hair.

"We're not done until I say we're done," he replied. "We haven't escaped the Gloria Furore, I'm not home on Centurios, and the real Captain Hellemut is out there somewhere, seeking vengeance."

Anguissa kissed him quickly. "That's *your* quest. Mine was to help my sister and my ship escape Hellemut, and to claim the Seed." She pulled on her boots then turned to face him. "That *is* done. Time to see if I can charm my father into letting me have the Archangel back."

Time to check on that cargo and verify that the robot had kept Thalina safe from it.

It was all perfectly clear to her and Ryke was certainly too sensible to disagree.

If he thought she needed the fiction of a relationship to feel good about what they'd just done, he could think again.

He looked uncertain, though.

Anguissa turned around and sniffed, certain she could smell something edible. "Did you say there was food?"

Ryke folded his arms across his chest and blocked the portal. "Claim the Seed," he echoed. "You mentioned the Seed before. What *exactly* does that mean?"

"What do you think it means, Ryke? I messed up on the deck of the Armada Seven, because I smelled the Seed. I made a mistake for the first time, because I smelled the Seed for the first time."

"What does that mean?"

"I had to identify the Carrier of the Seed, which was you, as soon as possible."

"Was?" His eyes narrowed.

"Was," Anguissa agreed. "The Seed has been claimed or have you already forgotten what we did here?"

Ryke took a step closer, backing Anguissa into a wall. His voice was a low, taut monotone. "Why did you need to claim the Seed?"

"Oh really, Ryke. There can only be one reason. Basic biology doesn't vary that much, regardless of species. It takes two, or sometimes more, but for our physiology, two will do." She smiled at him cheerfully. "We have that in common."

He didn't smile in return. "Tell me about the Seed," he demanded, grinding out the words. His eyes were dark and his manner was particularly grim.

Even for Ryke.

Anguissa folded her arms across her chest, facing him squarely. "My kind do not reproduce often or easily. In fact, we can only conceive when we encounter the Carrier of the Seed, a destined biological partner. We have an ability to smell the Seed and a primal urge to claim it, which means that the need to seduce the Carrier of the Seed distracts us from everything else until that seduction is done."

"And then?"

"And then it's *done*. The Seed is claimed, the child conceived, the Carrier and dragon shifter can go their separate ways."

"Then you've conceived my child?" he asked. "Already? How can you be sure?"

"Because I can't smell the Seed the same way. It's not messing with my thoughts, which means mission accomplished." She patted him on the shoulder as he glowered at her. "You don't have to worry about any future responsibility, Ryke. I'll take care of everything."

"Boy or girl?"

She was surprised that he cared. "It's even money, I'd say."

"Shifter or not?"

"Usually shifter, but the genetic string that defines my kind is occasionally elusive."

"*Umbro* or not?"

"No idea." Anguissa smiled at Ryke, who was as humorless as she'd ever seen him. "Maybe your genetic stock will feel the need to dominate, just the way you do." She tried to step past him but he made a little growl and stayed put.

Anguissa felt the need to provoke him a little, since he was so determined to decide everything. She tipped her head back to meet his gaze. "Or maybe, you need to be dominant because you're not as confident as you'd like me to believe. An over-compensation of a kind." She considered it for a moment, then shrugged. "I'll never know. Point me to food and then the chart room."

"You're not leaving me," Ryke said flatly.

"I'm not staying with you."

"You're not leaving if you've conceived my child."

Anguissa returned his glare. She'd humored him enough and she felt her snakes starting to sway in agitation. "You can't stop me," she said and heard the snakes hiss.

Ryke looked as if he wanted to try, but he paused to survey her.

Then he raised his hands in abrupt surrender. "Let's eat first," he said and she regarded him with suspicion. Either he was offering a truce, or he thought he could distract her from her goal.

Not a chance.

"How hungry are you?" he asked.

"Starving."

"Good, because Bakiel should be awake by now."

Bakiel?

"Who's Bakiel?" Anguissa wasn't really surprised that Ryke ignored her question. "More importantly, is there anything decent to eat? Even freeze-dried provisions would be good at this point."

"I can do so much better than that, Snake-Eyes."

She eyed him, liking his smug smile and his conviction that he knew exactly what she wanted. It would almost be worth staying to have a chance to surprise him and shake his assumption a bit.

It would almost be worth the temptation of doing what Ryke wanted, just to have the opportunity to give him that lesson about a dominant lover.

Almost but not quite.

Chapter Four

nguissa leaving?

There was absolutely no chance of that happening.

Not if it was true that she carried his child.

Ryke had already been compelled to abandon one son and he wasn't going to do it again. He wasn't sure he believed Anguissa, or if she was just trying to manipulate his thinking. Either way, he couldn't let her leave until he knew for sure whether she carried his child.

How was he going to convince Anguissa to agree? He'd never met a woman who believed she could do whatever she wanted, much less one who welcomed the responsibility for everything.

While it was true that Captain Hellemut was female, Ryke didn't think of his former commander as a woman—and even she had relied heavily upon other members of the team. Hellemut had a tendency to assume that the details would be managed, and to enjoy the allotment of punishment when it didn't. He'd long suspected that her command was lazy because she preferred torment over precision.

Anguissa was different. She took charge and seemed to like it. He'd never met a woman he found so persuasive, and that worried Ryke. Were all the old Centurion stories about dragons true? The worrisome thing was that even if they were, he couldn't imagine exterminating Anguissa.

Was that proof of her power over him?

Ryke changed the subject to give himself time to strategize.

Fortunately, Anguissa was interested in food.

They left the captain's quarters together and Ryke indicated the route to the canteen. Anguissa's stomach rumbled audibly in anticipation and he found himself reassured that some things about her were easy to understand.

She spared him a glance and he braced himself for something unpredictable. "You married, Ryke?"

He shook his head. Was that the reason for her concern? He'd discovered in his research that the dragons of Incendium tended to be monogamous. Although he'd never shared that inclination—it wasn't common on Centurios—it was easy to believe that Anguissa wouldn't share. *Umbros* of power didn't share either. They kept harems of princesses so they could choose which one to enjoy on any given night, but the women weren't shared with anyone else.

"In a committed relationship?"

He gave her a look. "You do remember the bit about the Gloria Furore?"

"But you might have been before that."

Ryke shook his head once more.

"Then here is an example of cosmic injustice," she said and he couldn't read her tone. Was she mocking him? He wasn't used to that.

"How so?" he asked warily.

"You're gorgeous, Ryke. You're strong. You're a great pilot and an effective warrior. I suspect you're noble and you're certainly courageous."

"I'm going to guess that you think flattery will get you something."

"It's just the truth." She patted him on the arm. "I'm trying to address your terrible lack of confidence." Ryke rolled his eyes. "By your own admission, you don't even make mistakes."

"That's your claim, too."

Anguissa ignored that and kept talking. "You make love like you invented it, at least given the limitations of your favored style of lovemaking—"

"Limitations?" he echoed in a low growl.

Her smile flashed. "And you know when to offer food. I admit that you do have this confidence problem, and there's the pesky matter of you being an *umbro*, but where is the line of women prepared to serve you forever and bear your sons?"

So, she was competitive.

That he could understand.

"They're on Centurios," he admitted.

"Didn't bring a couple of them along, just to service your needs?"

"Abductions don't work like that."

"Would you have?"

Ryke shook his head. "I didn't want any of them and I had the right to choose."

"Do you think you're choosing me, then?" She seemed to think this was a joke, which mystified Ryke. Given his lineage, he was always the one to choose.

"I will choose you, since you intend to bear my child."

Anguissa shook her head, setting those snakes in motion. "Not good enough, Ryke. Both people need to choose to be together, and it has to be for something more than obligation."

"There is nothing more important than responsibility!"

She leaned closer, those flames in her dark eyes. "What about love?"

Ryke scoffed. He couldn't help it. "A fiction," he said and immediately saw that they'd found a point of disagreement.

"Then the sooner we part the easier it will be," Anguissa concluded and continued ahead of him. "I knew an *umbro* couldn't be my HeartKeeper. Glad to have that resolved."

Ryke felt his eyes narrow. "What makes you think you can be the one to decide?" he demanded as he strode after her.

Anguissa laughed. "I always choose my destiny."

"No." Ryke shook his head. "When it involves me and my child, *I'm* the only one with the right to choose." He gave her an intent look, but knew better than to hope for an easy agreement.

"The right to choose?" Anguissa echoed, her tone thoughtful. "Why does that sound important?"

"Because it is, obviously."

"Why?"

Ryke spun to confront her. "I choose my destiny and that of everyone bonded with me. It's not complicated, Snake-Eyes."

"But what gives you that power?"

"It's my birthright," he admitted without meaning to do so.

Anguissa regarded him with curiosity. "What birthright? Who *are* you, Ryke? A king among *umbros?*" She ran her fingertips over the inside of her left arm and frowned. He realized she had a thin screen mounted there, adhered to her skin, but it wasn't illuminated.

Did she intend to research him?

It was Ryke's inclination to end the conversation, but he had an idea. Maybe he could spark that curiosity of hers, by *not* answering many questions, and ensure that Anguissa stayed with him. It wouldn't work for long, but it might work for long enough.

He turned away from her and continued to the canteen. "I told you my name. If you want to know more, you should come to Centurios with me."

Anguissa laughed so hard that he glanced back. "Oh, Ryke, Centurios is the last place in the universe I'll ever go."

"But that's where we're going."

"No, that's where *you're* going. Not me. I have a personal policy of not visiting systems or planets where my kind are considered to be abominations that have to be exterminated." She smiled. "How else do you think I managed to survive more than three hundred of years in command of a vessel?"

Three hundred years?

Ryke glanced back, intrigued. Had he met his match? "How old are you?"

"Almost four hundred Incendium years. Three ninety-six, actually."

"How many children have you had?"

"None." She was impatient with the question. "I only just met you, Ryke, and you're the Carrier of the Seed. It's not that complicated." She mimicked his earlier tone perfectly, her eyes sparkling. "I can explain it again if you like. Maybe more slowly."

"Let's eat," Ryke said crisply instead and turned to march to the canteen. How was it that Anguissa could both irritate him and entice him? She didn't seem to take anything seriously, she teased him—which no one had ever had the audacity to do before—she defied him, and oh, she tempted him.

If he hadn't been starving, he might have cast her over his shoulder and gone back to the captain's quarters, just to show her (again) who was in command.

Once might have been enough to deliver the Seed, but it certainly hadn't been enough to satisfy him.

Of course, he'd been with the Gloria Furore for what

seemed like an eternity.

"Why didn't you want any of them?" Anguissa called after him.

Ryke knew exactly who she meant.

"They were all princesses," he muttered.

"I'm good with princesses." Anguissa clearly felt a little insulted. Ryke could hear it in her tone.

Maybe that was why she riled him so much. Maybe it was a trait of dragon princesses. It certainly wasn't a trait of the other princesses he'd known, all of whom had been languid, dumb, and disinteresting.

Especially in contrast to Anguissa.

"I'm not," he said flatly.

"And why was it up to you to choose, Mr. Birthright? Whose son are you?"

Ryke was fed up. "I had the right to choose because that's how Centurios works, *Snake-Eyes!*" he roared then wondered if she'd cry.

Anguissa scoffed instead. "Men make all the decisions? I like the idea of your world less all the time. You definitely need drop me off somewhere else on the way. Food first, then the chart room." She gave him a playful smile and entered the canteen, her hips swinging with a sensual promise that made Ryke hungry.

And not for food.

"You should remember that there are other advantages to staying on board," he murmured when she was alongside him. He could smell her scent and feel the heat of her skin. It was easy to remember her wrapped around him, demanding more, and his body responded immediately to the memory.

"Like?" She looked up at him, lips curved in a smile, eyes dancing.

Daring him.

Ryke seized her around the waist, picked her up and backed her into a wall. "Me," he said with resolve. "I'll be here." He kissed her before she could reply, bending all of his will upon seducing her.

Anguissa didn't fight him.

No, not this woman. She welcomed sensation and pleasure, and then demanded more. She melted with a little sigh of capitulation, then arched against him, seizing a fistful of his hair, rubbing herself against him, setting his very soul on fire. Her tongue did magical things to his resolve, like melting it. Ryke was beginning to wonder what it would be like to let Anguissa ride him, if it would be worth it to let her take command of their lovemaking, if he would survive the fire she would incite.

But that would be wrong.

It would be a violation of all he knew to be right.

It would be, in fact, an abomination.

No, she liked being taken just the way he did it. Hadn't she begged for it? She might talk a lot of nonsense—probably just to provoke him—but she liked how he loved her just fine.

He'd been right about that.

Ryke broke their kiss and set her on her feet, knowing there was satisfaction in his expression as he looked down at her. Anguissa sighed, her lashes fluttering as she leaned against him in complete surrender.

Ryke felt a glow of satisfaction. This was more like it. He *was* right. He knew what she wanted better than she did.

"I *choose* you, and I will make it worth your while. Now, let's eat." He turned to stride into the canteen, confident that she would follow submissively behind.

She'd admitted she was hungry, after all.

Ryke's expression was so smug that Anguissa couldn't let the moment pass unchallenged. His kiss had been amazing, but the man needed a correction to his thinking if he believed she was going to be an obedient little female for whatever duration of time they were going to enjoy together.

She lowered her gaze so he wouldn't glimpse rebellion in her eyes. Her snakes hissed a little but he ignored them, seeing what he wanted to see.

How like a man.

Truth be told, she was disappointed in this side of his nature.

When Ryke continued into the canteen, obviously expecting her to follow at his heels like a trained pet, Anguissa waited only a moment before she tackled him from behind. She tripped him, rolled him to his back and pinned him down on the floor of the canteen. Ryke was surprised and not entirely pleased.

"Now, *I* choose," Anguissa said before he could argue, then kissed him leisurely and thoroughly. This part of his nature worked just fine for her. She held him down, taking what she wanted, feasting upon him at her own leisure. She waited until she could feel the enthusiasm of his response, then lifted her head.

"That's how things work on Incendium, Ryke," she informed him. "The royal family of dragon shifters chooses, and men do what they're told." It wasn't entirely true, but she enjoyed provoking him. Ryke's eyes flashed, but Anguissa rolled easily to her feet. "Clearly, we aren't each other's HeartKeepers and shouldn't even risk visits to our respective worlds. Is there food or not?"

She pivoted to find a stranger watching them from the other side of the canteen. He was tall and thin and remarkably pale. His hair was so blond as to be nearly silver, his skin was white and his eyes were as clear as water. She wasn't sure they had a color at all.

He looked a bit astonished by the sight of her.

Anguissa smiled and stepped forward, offering her hand. "You must be Bakiel," she said in the universal tongue.

The man's eyes widened and he took a step backward. Was it her imagination that he wavered a little, as if he was made of mist?

"She's a dragon shifter princess, Bakiel," Ryke growled from behind her. "It's easier to humor her, as you've just seen."

Bakiel hurried forward and took Anguissa's hand, barely touching her before he retreated again. His hand had been cool and soft, so fragile that Anguissa had the sense that she could have crushed it easily.

Maybe he sensed the same thing.

Maybe that was why he was keeping his distance.

"Your *luxa*?" he whispered to Ryke, who scowled.

"No!"

"What's a *luxa*?" Anguissa asked. Bakiel averted his gaze but Ryke glared at her.

"A myth." He seated himself at the table and Anguissa loved that he looked both disoriented and a little disheveled. His eyes glimmered as he watched her and she guessed that he hadn't liked that she'd tackled him in front of his friend.

He should get used to it.

What an unlikely pair Ryke and Bakiel were. She was struck that they appeared to be such opposites, but the bond between them was almost tangible.

"Brothers?" she guessed. "Lovers?" Although the first seemed unlikely, she had a feeling the second would annoy Ryke if she said it aloud—which was why she had.

He caught his breath and she hid her smile as he glared at her.

"Friends," Ryke said firmly, although it took him a moment to choose the word.

Anguissa eyed him. There was more to this relationship than friendship, she could smell as much, and she was going to find out what it was.

Whether Ryke wanted to confide in her or not.

The way she saw it, she had to know more about Bakiel to know whether he was trustworthy. It was a matter of self-defense.

Maybe he had recoiled because he was from Centurios—where her kind were abhorred.

Or maybe there was more.

To Ryke's relief, Bakiel *was* awake and, just as Ryke had hoped, his old friend was cooking. Bakiel could do magic with provisions and when he was on Centurios, his culinary skills were completely unsurpassed.

That wasn't Bakiel's official role in Ryke's life, of course, but it was a welcome talent. When Ryke came out of a slip, he was always ravenous. Bakiel had made an art of cooking while standing guard.

Ryke was glad that Bakiel didn't look any worse for wear after his time in stasis. As far as he could see, his *custo* hadn't been injured in any way, either, which had been his fear all these years. Bakiel was several years older than Ryke, born to a lower caste, but they'd known each other almost all their lives—they'd been bonded young, and become friends, too.

"I knew you'd turn up hungry," Bakiel said by way of greeting. "The universe revolves around certainties such as this." He'd put the stew into zero-gee modules, probably because he wasn't sure of Ryke's plans. Bakiel hated a mess. Ryke appreciated that, but would have preferred eating from a bowl.

Soon enough, he'd be back on Centurios, with Ryko Primus, and be able to indulge in all its familiar pleasures.

What about the pleasure of Anguissa's company? Ryke had a feeling he might be living without that, and he didn't like it one bit.

He had to change her mind.

Somehow.

Was she telling him the truth about the Seed? It

seemed incredible, but then, the universe was full of facts that were hard to believe.

"How'd you sleep?" he asked Bakiel.

"Well enough. It was chilly, and I had some weird dreams, but hey, all is good." Bakiel held up his hands. "Seven years later and I've only aged a couple of minutes. Who can argue with that?" He eyed Ryke. "You didn't..."

Ryke interrupted him before he could finish the question. "Never without you, my friend."

Bakiel was visibly relieved. Anguissa's curiosity was almost tangible. Bakiel nodded toward her. "Another concubine?"

Anguissa straightened and her snakes hissed, which didn't surprise Ryke one bit. Bakiel retreated in obvious alarm.

"Princess Anguissa," Ryke said, pointing to her. "Bakiel," he told her, indicating his friend.

"She's almost as pretty as Mareeqa." Bakiel said, as if Anguissa wouldn't be able to hear or understand him. Ryke could have wished for that.

"Almost?" Anguissa echoed quietly, her snakes hissing a little louder as they writhed in agitation. "And who is or was Mareeqa?"

Ryke glared at Bakiel, who wasn't going to answer anyway. He was staring at Anguissa. Ryke doubted his friend had ever seen anything like those snakes. Or maybe he'd never confronted a woman who was so forthright.

"It's not important," Ryke said tightly.

"It or she?" Anguissa asked, her gaze simmering.

Ryke didn't answer. He was well aware that Anguissa was simmering. She wasn't used to being denied anything. On one hand, he figured it would be good for her to learn that she wasn't in charge everywhere.

On the other hand, any denial or perceived insult might convince her to leave him more quickly.

Ryke's gut clenched at that prospect.

"She," he replied, then turned to Bakiel as Anguissa's eyes narrowed. "What'd you make?" He had to hope his questions about Anguissa would have better answers when he wasn't so hungry.

Bakiel served Ryke with an apologetic shrug. "I found pretty much everything for the stew, even the spices. I know you hate the tubes, but a person only has to clean dinner out of a ventilation system once to never want to do it again."

Ryke took a taste, not surprised to find it delicious. "It's great. You always could improvise better than anyone else. Thanks, Bakiel."

"Are concubines and princesses to be seen and not heard?" Anguissa asked. "Are they permitted to eat in the company of a man with such a birthright?"

Bakiel was clearly startled by her tart tone. He looked between Anguissa and Ryke, obviously not knowing what to do.

But then, he was from Centurios.

"Women eat last on Centurios," Ryke explained.

Anguissa shook her head. "Tell me again why you thought I'd want to visit your home planet?"

"Because I choose for you to do so."

Anguissa smiled and folded her arms across her chest. "So I can meet Mareeqa?"

"Oh, that won't happen," Bakiel said under his breath, falling silent when Ryke gave him a poisonous glance.

Ryke stood, abandoning his meal, and prepared another portion for Anguissa. He set it down on the table and resumed his place. He could feel Bakiel's astonishment. "Sit," he invited Anguissa. "Eat."

"I might be too overwhelmed by your gallantry," she said.

"You're probably too hungry for that."

"You're right," she said, flashed him a smile, then sat down and began to eat. "This *is* delicious," she said to Bakiel, who watched her warily. "Thank you very much."

"Is she talking to me?" Bakiel asked.

"She's not talking to the food storage unit," Ryke replied. "I don't think it's smart enough to reply, and she doesn't like robots or automatons anyway."

"Why wouldn't I talk to you?" Anguissa asked. "Why wouldn't I thank you?"

"Princesses don't talk to anyone other than their keepers," Bakiel said. "And my caste is only qualified to serve..."

Ryke cleared his throat.

"Ryke's caste," Bakiel concluded hastily.

"And what is Ryke's caste?" Anguissa asked. He supposed it was predictable that she picked out the most important detail so easily. "King of the *umbros*?"

Bakiel's eyes widened again.

"It's not important," Ryke said, surprised to find that Anguissa said the words along with him. Bakiel was watching them, obviously both fascinated and shocked. "Flame Thrower," he added.

"Soul Stealer," she replied.

"Fire Face."

"Host Killer."

"Worm Scale."

"Shadow Vermin." Anguissa looked up. "Worm Scale?"

"Not my best choice."

"No. You're losing your touch, Ryke. Maybe it's food deprivation. You'd better eat up."

Ryke indicated Anguissa to the startled Bakiel. "This princess is a bit different from the ones you've known before."

Bakiel had apparently been struck dumb. He was watching the snakes of her hair, seemingly mesmerized.

"Call me Anguissa if it's easier for you," she invited. "Or Snake-Eyes."

Ryke almost smiled at that.

Bakiel swallowed. "Do they bite?"

"Only when I'm really angry. I doubt I could ever get sufficiently annoyed with you, but Ryke has already been bitten a couple of times. It's his gift."

"She likes me," Ryke told Bakiel.

Bakiel grinned at Anguissa's snort of disdain.

"We don't have castes on Incendium," Anguissa said when Bakiel remained standing. Obviously she'd noticed his deferential manner. "Come, sit, eat. Ryke will get over it. He's already eating with a woman and a princess, after all."

Bakiel hesitated only a moment, then came to sit opposite them. He didn't serve himself anything to eat. "Aren't there dragon shifters on Incendium?" he asked.

"You're talking to one," Anguissa said with a smile. "If you ever need something roasted a little more, Bakiel, just let me know."

"I couldn't allow it," he said quietly. "Not for Ryke's food."

Anguissa looked between the two of them, inviting an explanation.

Ryke ignored her.

"Why don't you like robots?" Bakiel asked Anguissa. "Princesses I've known have relied upon android service to keep from doing anything themselves."

"She's not your typical princess," Ryke reminded him.

"Not a typical princess from Centurios, that's for sure," Anguissa supplied. "What little I know about them isn't working for me."

"But why not robots?"

"Well, they're outlawed on Incendium, so I grew up with a natural aversion to them. Once I met a few, though, it became personal."

"Why?" Bakiel asked but Ryke was interested as well.

"They do what they're told," Anguissa explained. "Exactly what they're told, and I don't like that."

"Well, that explains why you like Ryke," Bakiel countered, relaxing in her presence. "He never does anything he's told to do. Why, his father..."

"Bakiel!" Ryke growled in warning.

Bakiel visibly bit his tongue and fell silent, his pale eyes flicking from Ryke to Anguissa and back.

No doubt about it. Anguissa had a dangerous power over Bakiel. The knowledge made Ryke wary.

"So, Ryke has a father," Anguissa said cheerfully. "That's unexpected news."

"Did you think I was hatched from a pod, Princess?"

"There's something about you, Ryke, that makes it hard to believe you're not completely solitary, that you didn't just spontaneously appear somewhere as, maybe, your birthright. But now I've met Bakiel, your friend, and I've learned that you have a father. Let me build up my strength a bit before you shake my assumptions again, please." Anguissa winked at Bakiel who grinned. He was obviously completely taken by her.

"Why is it an issue that robots do what they're told?" Ryke asked, curious that she'd list that as an issue. He would have thought she'd like obedience.

He did.

Anguissa finished her meal and sighed with satisfaction, treating Bakiel to a smile so brilliant that Ryke wished she'd smile at him that way. "Thank you again, Bakiel. That was wonderful."

The other man blushed.

Then Anguissa turned a bright glance upon Ryke. "Do you know anything about Argetan silicon?"

"Only that it's the best in the universe."

"And rare," Bakiel interjected. "Even the last I heard, it was really expensive."

"Exactly. Once upon a time, not so very long ago, I was hauling a load of Argetan silicon. It was a good contract, delivering the silicon from the mines on a distant moon in their system to the refinery on their home planet. The terms were fair and the price was more than excellent, to be paid on delivery."

Ryke sat back and guessed "But not without risk."

Anguissa shook her head. "No. The Gloria Furore had infiltrated the wormholes in their system and were raiding the deliveries. They were seizing the freighters and transiting them against their will, battling for custody of the ore in other systems, then ransoming the ore back to Argetan. The Argetans were quite honest about the risks when the contract was assigned."

"But you still took it."

"Oh yeah. Because there was also a bounty if the pirating raids by the Gloria Furore could be stopped."

"You didn't take them on?" Ryke was horrified.

Anguissa smiled. "I certainly did."

He shifted on his seat, not liking the sounds of this at all. It was one thing to have courage. It was quite another to spit in the eye of the most violent and vengeful league of space pirates ever known.

Pretty much the way he had just done. How exactly was Ryke going to ensure that he wasn't captured again?

Anguissa continued easily. "I'd met another pilot in the bar at a station frequented by freighters like mine. It doesn't matter where or when it was. The thing was that he told me about both the contract's availability and the Gloria Furore's scheme."

"Because he'd survived it."

Anguissa nodded. "Barely. He was retiring, heading back to his home planet to grow sprouts and watch the suns rise. He said he couldn't take the risk anymore."

"But you like risk."

"Love it. It proves to me that I'm alive." She smiled

slightly in recollection and Ryke knew exactly how she'd won that pilot's confidence. Something tightened within him but he knew it wasn't jealousy.

He was never jealous.

Of anyone.

"Did he let you be on top?" he asked without meaning to do so.

Anguissa's smile filled with such satisfaction that Ryke wished he'd been able to stay silent. "It's the best way," she purred. "Too bad you didn't let me show you. You might have been converted. Maybe you'll dream about it, Ryke. Or me?"

"I won't have to dream about you. You'll be staying with me."

Anguissa shook her head, her gaze unswerving. She was so convinced of her decision and her right to make it that Ryke didn't know how to argue with her.

He frowned and pretended to be fascinated by his meal. Truth be told, it tasted a whole lot less delicious than it has just moments before.

Anguissa continued her story with familiar confidence. "He told me where they went to fight over the payload."

"And you thought you could outsmart them," Ryke said with disgust. "Did it ever occur to you that he might have been one of their agents?"

"It did, but I was tempted. I went in, eyes open, took the contract and left the mining moon with my hold stuffed full of high-grade silicon. They came out of the wormhole exactly as he had said they would. We pretended to be surprised and let ourselves be taken. We were transported to the very same system that the pilot had told me would be their destination. It was on the end of a distant sector, an uninhabited system."

"No witnesses or chances of intervention," Ryke muttered, well familiar with the strategy. It was typical of the Gloria Furore to isolate their intended victims and leave few choices—except the one that would doom the victim.

"Except for one small detail," Anguissa said with satisfaction. "I'd made some preparations."

"What kind of preparations?"

"I had two Starpods in the hold of my ship, nice little numbers with heavily armored hulls and considerable artilleries. We released them as soon as we reached the target system and I teleported to a third that we'd left in orbit around a moon."

"Like junk."

"Just like. So, the freighter was piloted by a robot, programmed for the navigation, and otherwise empty except for the payload of Argetan silicon. I knew they'd try to take the ship for the silicon. To force them to make their attempt sooner rather than later—"

"Because Starpods don't have that much oxygen," Ryke contributed, knowing how the Gloria Furore liked to wait for that vulnerability.

Anguissa nodded, evidently aware of it, too. "To force their hand, so to speak, the nav system of the ship with the cargo was programmed to dive into the sun of the system."

"That trajectory was a feint to draw them out," Ryke said.

"It worked. They came fast. The fight was short and fierce. We lost one Starpod when it was annihilated and the other was taken by the Gloria Furore. They tried to ransom my crew to me, but we'd planned another feint. The crew teleported to my Starpod just before the capture."

"Much the way the Archangel jumped as soon as you were teleporting."

"Exactly."

"Risky business, princess."

Her eyes lit. "The very best kind. As soon as they took that Starpod into their hold, the bomb detonated."

"They must have known there was no one aboard."

"No, my co-pilot over-rode the sensor data to report that there were two lifeforms aboard, even though there were none. He had the ability to disguise the transport, too."

"He's good."

"Bond is very good," Anguissa agreed with an enthusiasm that made Ryke wonder at the full extent of their relationship. He refused to consider what she thought of Bond as a lover. "It wouldn't have stood up to a long scrutiny, but it didn't have to send the false signal for long. The Gloria Furore's ship sustained multiple damages and its hull fractured. We watched it go dark."

Ryke couldn't regret that any of the Gloria Furore had been exterminated. "And so you returned to your ship, delivered the silicon, and collected the reward, too."

Anguissa shook her head. "Not exactly. It was the robot, you see."

"I don't see," Bakiel said.

"It was imperative that the robot not know the full plan, in case the ship was taken before we won the battle against the Gloria Furore. In case they surprised us. So, the flight plan was to dive into the sun. Period."

"Oh no," Bakiel said.

"The last I heard from the robot was his congratulatory message on winning the battle against the Gloria Furore. We tried to send a message to change course, but the ship had entered the sun's magnetic field. All we could do was watch as the ship and its payload were incinerated."

Ryke couldn't even imagine how much that had cost Anguissa, in addition to the ship itself. No wonder she held a grudge.

"And that's why you hate robots?" Bakiel asked. "Because one made a mistake?"

"It wasn't a mistake, not in its perspective." Anguissa folded her arms across her chest. "Robots do what they're told. Nothing more and nothing less. A truly sentient being would have seen that we had triumphed, known that we couldn't possibly want to destroy the valuable payload, and would have changed course."

"That lesson cost you a fortune," Ryke said.

"And a whole lot of time," Anguissa admitted. "We were in the back of beyond in a Starpod that wasn't equipped for jumping. We had to wait for someone to come out of the wormhole and help us, ideally someone who was not the Gloria Furore."

Ryke knew the probabilities against that. "Let me guess. Your pilot friend and informant decided to stop growing sprouts."

Anguissa smiled. "He sent his daughter after us, afraid he'd steered me into trouble. She was a pilot, too."

Ryke was thinking about the long memories of the Gloria Furore and that his escape might be considerably more complicated if the space pirates were hunting both him and Anguissa.

Then he thought of worms in nav systems.

"What if it wasn't the robot at fault?" he asked and Anguissa turned to face him.

"What do you mean?"

"What if someone wanted you to lose the payload? What if there was a worm that overrode whatever command you gave the robot?"

"But who would do that? I trust my crew..."

"But one of them installed Hellemut's worm in the Archangel's nav system," he felt obliged to point out. "Was Bond present for both missions?"

Anguissa stared at him, then shook her head. "Yes, but it can't be him."

"Who else was on both missions?"

"Only Bond," she acknowledged, then shook her head. "It couldn't have been him."

"It could be anybody, Snake-Eyes," Ryke said gently. He admired her faith in her crew, but such loyalty wasn't always deserved.

"No! I've known Bond for half of forever." Her snakes were writhing, more agitated than Ryke had ever seen them. He knew it was a sign that she was shaken by his suggestion. "He's from Incendium. I trust him completely."

"Maybe that's not such a good idea. Everyone can be bought."

"No," she said, pushing to her feet. "No. You're wrong about Bond." She strode to the portal of the canteen. "Now, where's your chart room? I want to see your course and choose my own."

Ryke wasn't fooled. He'd startled her and challenged the trust she had in her crew. In her place, he would have denied the possibility, too.

But he could almost hear Anguissa thinking, sorting through her memories and searching for any details that correlated with the suspicion, either way.

Given time, she'd either build a case for Bond or against him.

Ryke was prepared to wait.

He was even prepared to argue his suspicion with her again, especially if it meant she didn't leave him just yet.

Not Bond.

It was impossible that Bond could have betrayed her.

But even as Anguissa fought against Ryke's suggestion, she was remembering little incidents that hadn't seemed important at the time. Bond insisting that he should have the entire suite of passwords to the Archangel, "just in case." Bond out of sight when she expected him to be on deck when they confronted the Armada Seven. Bond averting his gaze, as if he had a secret.

A secret he was ashamed of.

Bond having friends in every port. Bond needing to meet up with those friends to catch up on old times as soon as they docked.

Not friends. *Contacts.* Bond had to report.

He'd been first off the Archangel on Incendium. Did the Gloria Furore have spies there? Here she'd believed his story that he had kids on Incendium. A family she'd never met or even seen. Did they exist?

Not Bond, she thought fiercely, even as she acknowledged the spy probably had been her trusted crew member.

What had been his price?

She left the canteen with her thoughts churning, and guessed that the chart room was between her current position and the deck. She heard Ryke following her but didn't look back. She could do without any commentary on making another mistake.

It was a bit irritating how she kept showing herself badly in his presence.

Had that mistake been due to the Seed, too? No, she hadn't been able to smell it during that first encounter, not from the deck of the Archangel. She'd been aware of Ryke, though, behind Captain Hellemut on the display of the Armada Seven's deck, looking like a very tasty male specimen. She'd been aware of the censure in his intent gaze, too, but had thought at the time it was because he was truly allied with the Gloria Furore. They despised everyone who wasn't on their side.

She hadn't even smelled that he was an *umbro*, not then.

But his disapproval had been because she was a princess.

And not a passive one.

Anguissa turned when she felt a familiar tingle on the back of her neck. She turned and looked toward the deck. "The teleport is in use," she whispered.

Ryke frowned. "No, it isn't."

"Yes, it is," she insisted. "I heard it. I felt it."

Ryke looked annoyed, probably because she corrected him. "You can't possibly feel or hear the teleport from here and it's locked down."

"I heard it."

"Impossible."

"We have company, Ryke."

"We do not. You're getting jumpy." He tapped the comm, his gaze locked with Anguissa's. "Piper Twelve, has anyone boarded the ship without authorization?"

"Of course not, sir. The teleport is locked down."

Ryke spread his hands, smug again. "Thank you, Piper Twelve." He indicated a portal to the right. "Here," he said. "Forget the teleport and have a look at this." He entered an access code and the door slid open to reveal an old-style chart room.

Anguissa caught her breath. It was as magical as she'd always believed such rooms must be.

"I've never seen one," she breathed as she stepped into the darkened room. "Except on the hologram and it's not the same."

"Not even close," Ryke said with satisfaction. He stood inside the door, arms folded across his chest, watching her.

"Don't look so proud of yourself," Anguissa chided. "You didn't invent it just for me."

"No, but I'm showing it to you."

"Leaving me to wonder what you want in exchange," she replied, then examined the room without waiting for his reply.

Bakiel slipped into the chart room behind them, as

silent as morning fog, and surveyed the display.

Anguissa was fascinated. Although the chart room obviously had fixed dimensions, it didn't appear to have any walls at all, much less a floor. Within it was a projection of the known universe, in all its glory, an interactive and three-dimensional map.

She felt like she was stepping into space itself, though it was actually just a model. The chart room seemed to be filled with glittering dust, spaced at wide intervals. Each speck of dust was a star, and when planets circled that star was the sun at the center of a system, even smaller darker dots rotated around it.

"All this variety," Anguissa whispered, awed as she always was when she considered the universe.

"And more unknown," Ryke said. He tugged on the glove with pointers embedded in the tips of fingers and thumb, and made a gesture. The depiction of the universe swirled, then one sector zoomed larger. She felt as if they dove into that sector and heard Bakiel catch his breath in awe. Everything within it was magnified, the suns becoming larger and brighter, and the planets more visible. She narrowed her eyes and studied the closest system, certain she could even see a few moons.

She wasn't familiar with this quadrant at all. When Ryke reached out with his gloved hand, names appeared above systems and suns in the script of the universal standard language. Mytholos. Arkadeen. Krakaken. Names Anguissa had heard but locations she knew little about.

When Ryke moved his gloved hand, known wormholes glimmered in the proximity of this fingers, like lines of stardust. Some were brighter than others and she guessed that these were the clearer routes. There was a path illuminated in bright yellow light, and Anguissa knew this was their charted course. As Ryke had said, there were two more wormholes selected for jumps, but they didn't look short to her.

"So, that's Centurios?" she said, indicating the end point of the path.

"No!" Ryke responded, to her surprise. "This is all wrong!"

Chapter Five

o." Ryke strode across the chart room and back to Anguissa's side, his annoyance clear. "This isn't the course I programmed at all."

"Are you sure?"

He glared at her. "Of course, I'm sure! I don't make mistakes, Snake-Eyes." He strode across the hologram, indicating a system. The word "Centurios" appeared above the largest planet in that system. Anguissa looked left and right. That planet wasn't anywhere near their apparent destination.

Bakiel moved away from the wall, his concern clear. "Where are we going?" he asked. "And why?"

"So, that's why the jumps aren't so small," Anguissa mused. She went to the end point. "Formican," she read from the displayed label, answering Bakiel. He looked shocked.

"No!" Ryke said. He was furious. "I don't understand how this can be. Did you touch the nav?"

"Of course not!" Anguissa was thinking. She spun to face him. "How exactly was it that you were given the job of placing this freighter in its storage orbit around that moon?"

"It wasn't easy, Snake-Eyes." He averted his gaze.

"You did what an *umbro* does," she guessed. "You invaded the mind of someone in a position of influence, and once you were done, he or she died, bleeding from all orifices."

Ryke frowned. "No. That would have been obvious and I'd told them I wasn't an *umbro*. That would have shown I was lying to them."

"I can smell what you are."

"They couldn't."

"Then how?"

"I can be persuasive, Snake Eyes."

Anguissa felt her eyes narrow. "I would never have guessed."

She could see that Ryke was uncomfortable talking about it, and Bakiel was surprised. "Why this ship?" she asked quietly.

Ryke shoved a hand through his hair. "Because Bakiel was in statis on it and I had to help him."

"You did that much for a friend?"

Bakiel dropped his gaze, hiding his thoughts. Anguissa suspected she was missing some detail about the relationship between these two but she didn't know what it was.

"Anyone would," Ryke said, trying to deflect the question.

She didn't know nearly enough about *umbros* or Centurios. It was a rotten time to be without her personal assistant. "Most *wouldn't*. Why, Ryke? Tell me!"

Ryke confronted her, his voice a low growl. She liked how he towered over her and that he was fearless in disputing anything with her. That didn't happen often to a dragon princess. "Because he was the only one who tried to help me when the Gloria Furore captured me. What kind of a person would abandon a friend who was that loyal?"

Anguissa liked that answer better than either of her suggestions or suspicions. "And no one knew of the connection between you?"

"Of course not!"

"And yet, this freighter was stocked with troops after you left it, troops programmed to attack you."

Ryke folded his arms across his chest. His eyes gleamed as he tried to solve the riddle. "They were probably programmed to attack anyone who boarded the ship, Snake-Eyes. That's the style of the Gloria Furore and one of their favorite defense mechanisms. I wouldn't have known about it, because it wasn't considered to be germane to the completion of my duties." He leaned closer. "They didn't know I planned to come back and steal the ship."

There was that, but Anguissa was still troubled. "Did you ever consider that your assignment to be the last one aboard this freighter might have been assisted by someone else, instead of the result of your own brilliant planning?"

"No, because it wasn't."

Anguissa shook her head. "I think anyone who knew anything about you would guess that you would try to save Bakiel, and that you would come back for him, and that you would try to use this freighter to return to Centurios."

"I'm not that predictable," Ryke said, though the heat had left his voice.

"No, you're honorable, Ryke, and that makes you predictable."

He looked particularly grim and Anguissa knew he was giving consideration to her conclusion. "Let's prove you wrong." He turned and called. "Piper Twelve!"

The android appeared in the doorway to the chart room, though it appeared to be reluctant to cross the threshold. "You summoned me?"

It didn't call Ryke "sir" this time, which gave Anguissa a very bad feeling.

"What happened to our course?"

"It was revised."

"Who revised it, Piper Twelve?"

"The commander in authority of the ship."

"But I'm the captain of this vessel..."

"No, Lieutenant, you have been outranked," Piper Twelve interjected.

"By whom?" Ryke demanded.

There was a familiar chuckle and one wall of the chart room illuminated, dimming the display of the chart and showing the deck instead. Captain Hellemut lounged in the captain's chair, smiling. She was as enormous and her smile as malicious as Anguissa recalled.

Was this another doppelganger, or the real Captain Hellemut?

Either way, this was who had arrived by teleport.

"We meet again, Ryke," she said. "But this time, you won't be visiting the deck."

"How..." Ryke murmured, but Anguissa touched his arm.

"Let me guess," she said to Piper Twelve. "There was no unauthorized use of the teleport because the commanding officer of the vessel used the teleport to board."

"Exactly," the android agreed.

"Robots," Anguissa said softly. "What's not to love?"

"You are under arrest, Princess Anguissa, for the willful destruction of the Armada Seven," Hellemut said. "And you, Lieutenant Ryke, are being relieved of your rank, not just for treason but for aiding in the destruction of the Armada Seven. You will be tried on Formican, if you live long enough to arrive there."

Ryke was particularly impassive, but Anguissa sensed that he was trying to hide his panic.

Piper Twelve spoke from the portal. "You will all be secured in the containment cells until arrival at our destination." The robot gestured and six androids marched into the room, weapons at the ready.

Anguissa wasn't going into captivity without a fight.

Ryke stepped ahead of Anguissa to defend her, an instinctive reaction. Bakiel was also behind him. He couldn't see how they had a chance of evading arrest, but he wasn't going meekly back to Formican and its moon.

Once had been more than enough.

If he died defending his *custo* and the mother of his child, that would be the most honorable solution.

As he moved, Ryke glimpsed a shimmer of blue light. The hair stood up on the back of his neck and he turned in time to see Anguissa shift shape. She breathed a torrent of fire at the android guards and flung him behind herself with one claw. It was shocking how easily she did it. Bakiel ran for the far side of the chart room.

Ryke slammed into the exterior wall from the force of her shove and scrambled to his feet. The androids divided into pairs, each pair targeting one of them. One pair scurried toward him. He was surprised that only one carried a weapon, but then he saw that the other had a syringe.

Not again.

He fought furiously then, but the weapon was a stun gun, and one shot took him to his knees. He was reeling and disoriented, his heart pounding hard enough to jump out of his chest. He tried to fight them off, but he felt the needle slide home and knew he was done.

Powerless.

Again.

Ryke raged against the sedative that had to be in the syringe, even knowing his struggle would only make it take effect faster. The androids backed away, leaving him there.

Confident in the result.

He decided he just might hate robots as much as

Anguissa did.

The pair confronting Anguissa carried energy beam casters, much like that on the deck of the Armada Seven. Ryke saw the green light at the end of their weapons, but they had no time to loose the energy field on Anguissa. Her shift had taken them by surprise. Anguissa reared up and snatched them both. She smashed them together between her claws, reducing both of them to spare parts with brute force. She flung the pieces into the corridor, and Ryke heard Piper Twelve depart in a hurry.

Bakiel gave a short cheer. He'd been seized by simple force and his hands were bound behind his back. One of his captors punched him in the face and the other punched him in the gut. Bakiel doubled over and fell. He didn't get up.

Ryke winced that he had failed his *custo*, again.

Anguissa breathed fire at the two androids responsible. They tried to duck beneath her but lost the battle. She destroyed them thoroughly and flung the parts after the two that had tried to subdue her. The last two androids fled for the portal and secured it from the other side. She breathed fire at the barrier and it glowed red for a moment but didn't open. She pounded on it just as the display of the planets disappeared from around them.

"What's happening?" Bakiel whispered, looking up warily.

"Jump," Ryke managed to whisper.

He was fighting against the drug he'd been given, but losing the battle. The ship lurched hard to one side, sending them slamming into one of the walls. He rolled head over heels and Anguissa was evidently shaken up enough that she shifted shape again.

She fell against him, then turned to look into his eyes. "What did they give you?" she asked, but Ryke couldn't speak. He managed to lift one hand, but it took a massive effort, and he could feel his eyes closing.

"A sedative," she whispered. "Why?"

"Prepare to jump," came the warning from the deck.

"To keep him from slipping," Bakiel provided and Ryke nodded at the truth.

Hellemut had figured out what he was, which meant his future looked grim.

There were four seats at one end of the chart room, which would have to do for the jump. Anguissa started to drag Ryke toward them but he shook his head. "Bakiel," he whispered.

"Responsibility first," Anguissa said, understanding him perfectly. She helped Bakiel to a seat and strapped him down, then returned for Ryke. Anguissa took the seat between them, reaching for the tool compartment after they were strapped in. He wished he could do something to help, but the fog was invading his thoughts.

Anguissa found a universal key and unlocked the shackles on Bakiel's wrists. He thanked her and rubbed the marks on his skin when he was released.

"Galactic convention," Anguissa said. "No prisoner endures a jump under restraint. I remember it, even if Hellemut doesn't."

The sedative rolled through Ryke's body, spreading lethargy.

To be powerless was Ryke's worst nightmare and one he'd never hoped to experience again. To be helpless devastated him. To be used as someone else wished, to be unable to change his fate, to be a victim and an underdog was the most wretched fate imaginable. He fought against his situation, even knowing that there was nothing to be done.

He'd been drugged, again.

He was captive, again.

He'd never escape the Gloria Furore alive. They'd threatened to disembowel him before his own eyes. They'd threatened to kill him slowly, slowly enough that he would feel every instant stretch to eternity, they'd started on that diabolical plan when Hellemut had taken a fancy to him.

He'd been sedated and broken but not so lost that he would risk using his natural gift. He was determined to convince them that he wasn't an *umbro*—because he knew that if he confirmed his nature, they would use him as a spy, to target and destroy the enemies of the Gloria Furore. They'd prodded and provoked him, hoping to compel him to try to save himself. Instead, Ryke's resolve had hardened to steel and he became determined to hide his legacy.

He was sure he'd convinced them.

He was sure it was the reason they'd stopped sedating him.

But now, he was being put under again. Hellemut must suspect his gift.

Would he be used or destroyed? Desperation flooded through Ryke.

Anguissa *knew* his truth. He hadn't told her nearly enough, and ironically, she was their only chance of surviving this ordeal. Ryke couldn't lift a hand or even a finger. He could barely blink. They'd given him enough to stop him but not to kill him—his heart was still beating, albeit slowly, and he was breathing, very slowly. He was just barely alive.

Not unlike stasis.

But his mind was awake and he was aware of everything around him.

He couldn't save himself. He couldn't change his situation. He couldn't even tell Anguissa what he knew.

She said she would be the mother of his second child.

Because of her dragon nature, slipping into her mind could be suicide.

Ryke had never been so conflicted about a choice. Invariably, he knew the right decision immediately, but—

like so much else about Anguissa—the situation left him torn.

Was it possible that Bakiel was right? If Anguissa was his *luxa* and if the old stories were true, she'd survive a slip, regardless of her nature. They'd be able to work together, that was how the fable went. Ryke had never believed it, but he was desperate for options.

Would *he* survive slipping into the mind of an abomination? Or would she—as those stories went—twist everything he knew to be true so that he couldn't discern fact from fiction anymore?

The strategy wasn't without risk for either of them.

But Anguissa embraced danger.

She also liked surviving certain death, and the prospect of celebrating that with her made the choice. Ryke had everything to lose and only one slender chance of success.

He was going to take it.

All he had to do was convince Anguissa that he was right.

Ryke slipped, not quite all the way into Anguissa's mind, but close enough that she would hear him at the virtual keyhole.

Knock knock, Snake-Eyes.

There was a voice in Anguissa's thoughts, a voice that sounded a lot like Ryke's.

She turned toward him, his face close to hers in the darkness, and found a knowing gleam in his eyes. *Ryke?* She thought the question.

Who else?

But...

The only way our child is going to get out of this alive is if you know what I know, and the only way that can happen is if you let me in.

Anguissa felt her eyes narrow. *Let you in?*

Give me access to your mind.

I thought an umbro *didn't need permission to slip.*

We don't but I'm asking.

Why?

You know why. Slipping isn't without repercussions for the host.

Anguissa arched a brow. *You're going to take charge of my mind and body, feed on my spirit, then leave me to die? And you expect me to agree? Not a chance, Ryke...*

He interrupted her with a savagery typical of Ryke. *I knocked,* Princess.

Her heart chilled. That was evidently important, which led to an obvious conclusion. *And you didn't have to?*

Ryke's grim tone was also familiar. *We never knock. I vowed a long time ago to be different.*

Because it's your birthright to go where you want, uninvited.

Slip, not go. We call it slipping. And yes, pretty much.

Anguissa stilled. *Who are you, Ryke?*

There was amusement in his reply. *Is the answer the price of admission?*

Pretty much.

You're no pushover, Princess. I like that. But you've almost guessed.

King of the umbros.

Something like that.

Anguissa realized that he'd agreed very easily, for Ryke, and felt her suspicion rise. What did he know that she didn't?

That we haven't got a chance otherwise. These are very long odds.

Anguissa was inclined to agree. *No tricks.*

Wouldn't risk it. You're the best ally I've got. She almost heard him chuckle. *Is danger really the spice of life? If so, this should be the obvious choice.*

Anguissa took a deep breath. It wasn't a joke. She could die. Her trust in Ryke could be misplaced. If she declined, though, he could just slip into her mind anyway. And given the situation, they were all as good as dead.

Danger it would be. *All right then. Come on in, Ryke, but don't make me regret this.*

The invasion chilled her mind and she couldn't suppress a shiver of dread. There was something wrong about him being there, and she felt his presence so keenly that her thoughts actually seemed crowded. She found herself compartmentalizing her memories, thoughts, and observations, as if she was locking away her own secrets to protect them from him.

Don't fight it. I'll be as unobtrusive as possible.

Anguissa forced herself to relax. *And then?*

And then we're going to jump. Get ready, Snake-Eyes. He paused and she wondered why. There was doubt in his tone when he continued. *I'm not entirely sure how this will work.*

His admission sent fear through Anguissa. *You said abominations can defy umbros.*

The upside is that it hasn't killed either of us so far, but we could still go insane.

Anguissa caught her breath. She knew that Ryke hadn't made the choice lightly and respected his understanding of the risks—and the possibilities.

We or me?

We, you, me—all combinations are possible. Sadly, I have no ability to see the future. Do you?

No and you know it.

His tone was wry and confident again. *True. I did peek.*

Anguissa swallowed and faced the facts. She wasn't going to think too much of having a ruthless *umbro* in her mind who could easily kill her. She was going to think about Ryke and what she knew about him, about the way he went back for Bakiel, about her conviction that he'd keep his word. She felt him waiting on her reply and let herself scoff. *And I let you in.*

He chuckled. *Exactly.*

They jumped and Anguissa lost awareness of her situation, just as she always did.

And then she found herself where she'd never been before.

In more ways than one. She guessed that she was visiting Centurios—and she was doing it by sharing Ryke's memories.

She watched avidly, wanting to learn as much as she could about her enigmatic partner.

The crowd was restless.

Hungry.

A network of corridors and rooms, even prison cells, ran beneath the seating of the massive forum in the capital city of Centurios. Even through the layers of rock, the shouts of the attendees could be heard. The stamping of their feet made the walls shake. The air was filled with their shouts and their bloodlust.

"They're turning them away at the gates," Bakiel said, his pale eyes flicking as Ryke checked his armor. There was a lot less of it than he would have liked, but there were regulations. "The stands are overflowing."

"They expect a bloodbath," Ryke murmured.

"I hope they don't get one."

"You're not alone in that, my friend."

"You don't have to do this, Ryke."

"Yes, I do." Ryke had no doubt. Without this fight, without *winning* this fight, he had no future on Centurios. "It's my father's challenge."

"But..."

"But after all these years of wanting the opportunity to prove myself, I can't argue over the details. I asked. He gave. It's his way."

Bakiel's lips tightened to a thin line, but he refrained from commenting. Ryke knew that his *custo* wasn't fond of the current emperor's tactics, but if he said as much aloud, particularly here, Ryke might not be able to defend him. He was glad that Bakiel kept quiet.

"One knife, one sword, one mace, one shield," Ryke said, turning before Bakiel. "It's all I get, so I'll have to make it do."

"They say it's a hydra."

Ryke eyed his loyal companion. "I didn't think they existed."

"Maybe not the best time to find out," Bakiel said, then gave Ryke an intent look. He offered a length of cloth, and Ryke considered all he'd been told about hydras.

Poisonous breath.

Deadly blood.

Regenerating heads.

They were abominations.

"That's just a myth," he said to Bakiel. "If its breath is really toxic, a bit of cloth won't save me."

"This bit will."

Ryke took the cloth and examined it. It was very soft, but so finely woven that he couldn't even see the threads.

"*Filters*," Bakiel mouthed.

Ryke supposed it couldn't hurt. He tied it around his face, covering his mouth and nose.

"You know, you could always slip..."

"No," Ryke said, stopping his *custo* before he finished the suggestion. "I made a vow to myself and to Ryko Primus and I'm not going to break it now."

"Even to survive?"

"I'll survive. This is just a fight. A spectacle. Nothing more and nothing less."

"I suspect it's a lot more than that," Bakiel muttered. "I'll be ready in case you change your mind."

Ryke smiled. "Standing over me in the arena with a hydra attacking? I wouldn't ask that of you, my friend."

There was a knock on the door, which ended their discussion. Ryke wasn't going to cheat and use his gift to slip into anyone. He was going to win.

In his father's view, only might made right.

They left the room together to find the corridor to the arena lined with gladiators. They were burly men of various heights, each tanned and fit, with an impressive number of scars. They wore the same minimal armor as Ryke—helmet, breast plate, boots, gloves, and a guard over the groin—albeit with variations of color and style. Some had blue tattoos. Some had long hair and others were shaved bald. The hue of their skin varied from pale gold through to black and shades of blue. All of their gazes were assessing as they surveyed him in silence. He expected them to despise him, a son of privilege come to play at the sport that was their life.

It wasn't a game, though.

It was his chance.

He could be killed, just as they could be killed each time they entered the arena. They had the danger in common. The difference was that victory would grant him the opportunity he craved, while their triumphs only ensured they could fight again the following day.

They might hate him for that, too.

He respected them, but didn't expect that to be mutual. He nodded to the first man then headed for the patch of sunlight at the end of the corridor and the impatient roar of the crowd.

"May Mercado smile upon you," the man said gruffly, and Ryke glanced his way in surprise.

"And upon you," he replied by rote, amazed when the man bowed.

"We are with you, sir."

Ryke was surprised by the honorary address. "All warriors on Centurios are equal," he said gently.

The gladiator smiled. "Some more equal than others,

sir." He gestured to his comrades, saving Ryke from commenting. "Centurios would prosper beneath your hand."

"I will endeavor to see that it does, if such opportunity comes to me," Ryke replied carefully. There was spies everywhere in his father's realm, and he would not see anyone condemned for treason.

Winning this day was only the first step in earning the succession from his father.

Ryke would win.

He bowed in turn. "Thank you for your kind words, sir."

He saw that the gladiator was as surprised by the use of the honorary address as Ryke had been himself.

When he turned, the gladiators had all swept off their helmets. They bowed as he drew alongside each one of them, one after another, the same blessing crossing their lips. Ryke's heart squeezed that they gave him this unexpected salute, and he paused on the threshold of the arena for one last backward glance.

"May Mercado smile upon all of you, in all the battles of your lives," he said, then pivoted and stepped out into the sunlight. Bakiel remained behind, of course, so Ryke was alone on the pounded dirt of the arena when he heard the metal grate drop into place, securing the exit. He didn't have to look to know that Bakiel was clinging to the bars, watching him, and that the gladiators were clustered behind him.

The arena seemed much larger than he remembered, vast beyond belief, and he could scarcely comprehend how many people were in the stands that rose around the perimeter. Tens of thousands, maybe hundreds of thousands, all screaming, all on their feet, all stamping and shouting.

His name. They were shouting his name.

"Ryke. Ryke. Ryke." It settled into a rhythmic

repetition, like the beat of a song, and Ryke walked to the middle of the arena, keeping pace with their cry.

He paused, turned, and identified the emperor's box. He bowed to his father and whoever else might be there.

"May Mercado smile upon you!" came a cry, and Ryke's heart stopped at the familiarity of the young voice.

Ryko Primus was here!

His gaze raked the crowd, the imperial box, and landed upon the boy at the emperor's side. His son's hair golden in the sun, his face alight with excitement, his energy almost impossible to contain. He waved with enthusiasm, and Ryke felt as if he'd been kicked in the gut.

His son was watching.

He had to win.

Then the metal grate at the far end of the arena was raised, the gate that secured the pit of the beasts. It was four times wider than the one Ryke had used to enter the arena, and five times as high. The crowd fell silent as something roared from within that pen.

It sounded wild and large—and angry.

The hydra erupted from the doorway, its seven heads turning this way and that as it surveyed the arena. The crowd gasped at the sight of it. The beast roared and its tail slashed the air. It was huge, far bigger than Ryke had imagined such abominations might be, and when its gaze locked upon him, his blood ran cold. He planted his feet against the dirt, gripped his shield and held his blade aloft as the creature advanced upon him.

Ryke's *son?*

His father, the emperor?

His *custo?*

Anguissa had questions for her questions, but Ryke's memory unfolded so quickly in her thoughts that she had no time to ask them. She was experiencing his memory,

not just seeing and hearing it, but sharing his thoughts—
at least as many as he did share. Knowing Ryke even as
little as she did, Anguissa guessed that what she could
hear of his thoughts was just scratching the surface.

Yet at the same time, her own mind was present,
observing and coming up with endless questions. She
hadn't had much time to think about it, but she would
have speculated that in slipping, Ryke's thoughts would
replace her own and that at best, she'd be able to observe
his memory. She'd anticipated that it would be like a
memory dump between androids and that she'd have to
review it later to make sense of it.

If he left her that opportunity.

I could push you out completely, Snake-Eyes. Ryke's
thought echoed within her own. *But it's not my way to wear
out my welcome.*

You mean you might need to come in again.

There was a thread of humor in his tone. *Anything is
possible.*

The arena was large and had a sand floor. There was
seating all around it, tier after tier of seating, packed with
observers. She couldn't even guess how many had
attended but there wasn't room for one more person—
which said a great deal about the appeal of the fight.
Even though the air was hot, there were twin fires
burning in massive brass bowls, one on each side of
arena at the midpoint. The sky was dark overhead. Ryke
had emerged from a door at one end and faced a much
larger metal grate at the opposite end.

The crowd chanted his name. Flowers fell from the
stands to land in the dirt around him. Halfway up the
stands on the left, she could see an elaborate platform of
gilded wood, with a striped canopy protecting its
occupants from the sun.

The imperial box.

She almost felt him catch his breath as the hydra

appeared. It was a fearsome creature, with seven heads and an enormous lashing tail. Its scales were dark silver but dulled, like tarnished metal.

Any battle tips would be appreciated. I lost. Badly.

Anguissa looked more closely. There was something wrong with the hydra. It looked hungry to her and there was desperation in its survey of the crowded arena. How long had it been in captivity? How much had it been fed? She could see its ribs and knew it hadn't been enough. A hydra needed water and she guessed it hadn't seen any in a while. She could also see some scabbed wounds on its belly, and one claw was maimed, as if it had been broken and hadn't healed properly. Its yellow eyes were dull, perhaps indicative that it had been drugged, and two of its heads swayed unsteadily.

The creature was dead on its feet.

Trust you to take its side. Ryke apparently could hear her thoughts, too. *Sympathy was a galaxy away for me.*

The crowd shouted when the hydra didn't move and someone threw something at it. Whatever it was bounced off the creature's back. A shudder ran down its length and it stood suddenly taller. It glared upward, its tail swished, then the gaze of its primary head locked upon Ryke.

Its eyes shone brilliant gold, filled with malice and fury.

Anguissa definitely felt Ryke shudder. She frowned, studying the hydra, which could have been a different creature than the one forced into the arena. It raged and thrashed its tail, snatching at spectators with its claws and invoking terror in the arena before it bounded toward Ryke.

What happened there?

It saw me, Snake-Eyes. Ryke's tone was impatient.

No. Something changed.

It's a hydra. Who knows how many brains it has?

Anguissa fell silent, not convinced.

Despite Ryke's trepidation, in the memory, he lifted his blade and stepped forward, daring the hydra with a roar. He was courageous, she'd give him that. The crowd cheered. The hydra bellowed, its other heads turning swiftly to focus upon Ryke. Two heads screamed as the creature moved toward him and the primary head bared its teeth, bending down to bite Ryke.

The crowd was on its feet, shouting encouragement to Ryke. That chant of his name filled the air and Anguissa understood that he was popular.

Why was the emperor's son fighting a hydra in the arena?

Ryke jabbed his sword into the hydra's mouth and black blood gushed from its tongue. It flowed quickly, making the sand slick beneath Ryke's boots. The hydra screamed, releasing a torrent of foul breath, confirming Anguissa's suspicion that it hadn't been fed well. It snatched, seizing Ryke with one claw and squeezing tightly. Anguissa could feel the pain in Ryke's gut as the crowd hooted in sympathy. He writhed in the creature's grasp, struggling against its grip, and managed to stab the hydra in one snout.

The hydra hurled him to the ground so that the breath was forced out of him.

Ryke didn't move, apparently stunned by the blow. The crowd fell silent, their agitation palpable. Anguissa noticed that the boy who was Ryke's son was pale, gripping the edge of the imperial box as he watched.

Oddly enough, there was no sign of the emperor. No, he was further back in the imperial box, and appeared to be sleeping.

Sleeping? While his son fought for his life?

His interest is only in triumph. Might makes right, and failures aren't worth his attention. I let him down. It stands to reason he wouldn't watch.

Anguissa didn't comment on that, though she understood that Ryke considered himself one of the failures, by his father's definition.

Stab up, Anguissa thought when the hydra's belly reared over him.

In the same instant, Ryke did drive his knife upward, but it was deflected by the scales, only managing to make a scratch and feed the hydra's wrath.

Further back, Anguissa thought. *Where the gaps between the scales are greater. Near the genitals.*

I don't even want to think about being stabbed in the genitals.

You're lucky you still have a chance to think at all. Anguissa watched the hydra rage at Ryke. He lost his knife when it reacted to his scratch upon its belly, the hydra seizing the blade and hurling it across the arena. Anguissa didn't think Ryke had enough space to swing his mace, but he managed it and the blow landed in one of the hydra's eyes.

The creature screamed, blood flowing from that eye, and Ryke swung again.

Its primary head was blinded, but that didn't stop it from biting in Ryke's direction. He was seized and held aloft, but waited until the second head turned before he swung the mace. It landed on the brow of that head, which crumpled to the ground.

Now, Ryke was the one who seemed to catch his second wind. The hydra dropped him and he ran to pick up his fallen sword. He had time to snatch it up and swing before the hydra pursued him. With impressive might, he sliced off one of the seven heads.

The crowd roared their approval. Anguissa heard drums beating and the chant of Ryke's name began again.

Seven more heads sprouted from the hydra's wounded neck, each of them as large as the original, each snapping and snarling, but Ryke was undeterred. He swung his mace and sliced with his blade, backing the hydra toward one of the bowls of fire. After another blow, it seized his mace and ripped it from his hand, casting it into the crowd. There was a scream from one of the observers and a gasp of horror—and Ryke made the mistake of glancing away from his foe.

Ryke! Anguissa screamed a warning just before the hydra attacked.

Ryke had thought his loss in the arena had been humiliating, but it was a thousand times worse to review his failure while Anguissa was sharing his memory. Despite what he knew about her nature, she was a woman—and it was only natural to want to impress her.

Not show himself to be a loser.

Slipping was a one-way transaction—the *umbro* witnessing and influencing the thoughts of the host—but just as he'd feared, it was different with an abomination.

A beast mind.

Unpredictable. Unruly. Defiant of all rules.

Not only had Anguissa shared his nightmare, but she'd conversed with him and shared the horror of his dream. He'd meant to share details of Captain Hellemut with her by slipping into her mind, not for her to learn of his failures.

Was it because they'd jumped sooner than had been his flight plan?

Or was it something else?

She couldn't be his *luxa*. Ryke shied away from the ridiculous explanation. She had to have manipulated his memory, or maybe even him.

Just as he'd always been warned.

Would she twist his recollection of what he knew to be true, and convince him that fiction was fact?

Ryke awakened in the chart room, damp with perspiration, still shaking from the memory of that day.

He'd spent months healing and rehabilitating, which had only reinforced his father's conviction that he was unworthy.

Anguissa's head was on his shoulder, her snakes completely still for once. Even knowing what he did, he found his body responding to her warmth and her scent. He wanted her, again, which was all the evidence Ryke needed that the old stories were true. Bakiel was snoring softly on her other side. Ryke made to retreat from Anguissa's mind, sure he could slip away while she was still recovering from the jump.

He was wrong.

Don't go. I have questions.

It doesn't say anywhere that I have answers, Snake-Eyes. Ryke knew he sounded as agitated as he felt.

Anguissa twisted to meet his gaze and he was struck again by her beauty. Her eyes looked different, though, her thoughts hidden from his view, and Ryke stared because he'd never seen her look that way. She was always open and honest, and only now did he realize how important that had become to him.

Had he taught her to be evasive?

Or had she simply appeared to be guileless? Was that a ruse?

He hoped not, then wondered what was the truth. He reached into her mind, only to discover that there were boundaries he couldn't cross. There were memories he couldn't access, and opinions he couldn't even approach. She'd locked him out of most of her mind.

Had he lost his abilities as an *umbro?* Slipping was an inherent skill. It was innate, inherited, known and not taught. He couldn't forget how to do it, even with years of not practicing.

No, the difference was Anguissa—and the shape of her mind.

She smiled. *My eyes look like yours, because you slipped into me.*

Ryke frowned. *I was taught that someone who knew what to look for could see a slipped soul.*

You're embarrassed.

Why wouldn't I be? You shouldn't have seen that...

And now I wonder why you're so cocky.

Ryke stiffened. *Because I am the best, I've always been the best. Top of the class. Tallest, strongest, brightest. I've worked hard for that, because it's right for the son of the emperor to be better than his peers. I've always won.*

Until the day it really mattered.

My father was humiliated. I couldn't blame him for that. He never spoke to me in public again. He relieved me of my imperial duties and took custody of my son, as was only right.

Anguissa was silent for a long moment. *You said 'we' never ask permission before slipping. Does that mean* umbros *in general or just those of your lineage?*

My father is the emperor. He has the right... Ryke's thoughts faded to silence as Anguissa shuffled through his own memories.

He was startled that she could do that, but had no time to ask. The host shouldn't have been able to review or revise his memories. Ryke was supposed to be the influence hers.

At the beginning, the hydra was weak. She showed him the hydra as it entered the arena and he had to agree with her assessment. Its manner did change, as if a jolt ripped through its body.

I told you. That was when it saw me.

No, Ryke. Anguissa showed his quick scan of the imperial box, but slowed it down, lingering on the sight of his father sleeping during the battle. *Who's that?* Her attention was fixed on her father's *custo*, Wayling.

Standing vigilant, his pale eyes fixed on his patron.

The conclusion was inevitable, if shocking.

Ryke's father had slipped during the fight.

While Ryke fought for his survival, while he struggled to prove himself, his father had slipped! Where had he gone? Why hadn't he watched?

Anguissa's attention returned to the invigorated hydra, the fury in its eyes and its sudden power. *Let me guess. Your father didn't want you to prove yourself worthy.*

Her conclusion was obvious and Ryke was shocked again. He wanted to defend his father and that man's high ideals, but he had no words.

His father had slipped into the hydra, purely to defeat him, and teach him a public lesson. To disinherit him for cause.

But not quite kill you. What a merciful emperor he is. Anguissa's tone was wry even as Ryke was reeling from her conclusions.

His father had betrayed him.

No! Impossible! He was his father's heir, his father's pride and joy. His father had supported him and seen him trained and given him every advantage...

Anguissa snorted. *Your father has his own agenda.*

She was doing it. She was twisting the truth and making him believe it.

Abomination! Ryke roared and recoiled.

Anguissa was a dragon shifter. He had been warned from childhood of the powers of such a creature. Ryke had always been skeptical of those stories, but Anguissa's ability to review his memories and manipulate them, as well as her attempts to change his thinking about his own father, were more than adequate proof.

Revulsion rose within him and he felt her flinch. She was right to be afraid. He should exterminate her, start the bleeding, and save himself while he could.

But did she really carry his child? What would be the child's nature? Ryke didn't care—he had to ensure the survival of his own child.

Anguissa had to survive so that the child would

survive.

If it existed.

He couldn't kill her until he knew for sure.

It could only be a mark of how much she'd meddled with what he knew to be true that the realization filled him with relief.

He'd have to pretend to believe her conclusions about his father.

Ryke took a deep breath, mustered his thoughts, and remained in Anguissa's mind.

All he had to do was get back to Centurios alive.

He hoped that he could keep his sanity—and his secrets—that long.

CHAPTER SIX

nguissa mistook the reason for Ryke's silence, probably assuming that he was devastated by the revelation of his father's betrayal.

I'm sorry to have shocked you so badly.

It's all right.

It's not all right! You think you're a failure and a discredit to your father, but you're wrong, Ryke. Look. Look at how they admire you. She showed him the gladiators honoring him, the ranks of cheering citizens awaiting him in the arena, the cheers when he struck a blow and the moans when he fell. She let him hear the chanting of his name and showed him the agitation of the crowd when he was defeated.

She was seductive. It was easy to think as if he believed her, because part of him did.

The other gladiators poured into the arena to kill the hydra, and he recalled watching it through the haze of his pain. They had taken it down so easily that he appeared to be even more weak.

But as Anguissa showed him that memory, Ryke looked at the creature's eyes. They were dull again, cloudy. It wavered on its feet as if it was already half-dead, restored to the feeble desperation it had shown at first.

Had that truly been the case, or had Anguissa

changed his memory? It wasn't consistent with what he had believed or remembered.

His father was on his feet in the imperial box, calling for the demise of the savage beast.

His hand on Ryko Primus's shoulder. Ryke remembered that.

Anguissa wasn't done. *Where were you when the Gloria Furore took you, Ryke?*

What difference does it make?

Indulge me.

I abducted Ryko Primus when I was forbidden to even see him. We were snatched on the way to our new life.

What a coincidence.

Ryke was impatient. It would look suspicious if he agreed to all of her suggestions. *It was bad luck, Snake-Eyes. I was in the wrong place at the wrong time. The Gloria Furore have launched raiding parties on Centurios for eons...*

She turned to watch him, understanding in her eyes. *So, it was just a coincidence that they kept only you, the son of the emperor, exactly when your father wanted to get rid of you?*

It sounded so obvious when she argued it that way.

It made him feel like a failure all over again.

And that redoubled his conviction that she was deceiving him.

And your son?

They ransomed him. My father paid the price.

But not for you?

No one pays ransom on an outlaw.

Ryke's fists clenched. He slipped from Anguissa's thoughts, needing to escape the treacherous skill she showed in manipulating his assumptions. He felt like a child, an amateur, an *umbro* inexperienced with slipping, instead of the master he knew himself to be. He'd achieved the highest rank of skill before being captured by the Gloria Furore and it wasn't something he was going to forget. Bakiel slumbered on beside him, oblivious thanks to the jump.

Anguissa rolled toward him, her hand on his cheek, and touched her lips to his ear. "Come back, Ryke," she whispered. "We still have to get out of this mess, and I'm not looking forward to being sold to the highest bidder. Come back, so I'll know what you know."

She pressed a kiss into his ear, a sweet slow kiss, sending an unwelcome surge of desire through him. He wouldn't have thought it possible that he could have responded to her touch, not here, not now, not when his mind was spinning, but he felt warm and reassured.

She was controlling him so deftly that he should have been terrified.

Instead, he wanted to trust her.

Ryke knew he was in trouble—and not just from Hellemut.

"I'll even let you be on top again," she murmured, laughter underlying her tone. That she could be amused when they were in such deep shit impressed Ryke. It wasn't that she was stupid. It wasn't that she failed to understand their bleak situation.

She was an optimist. A confident, charming, optimist.

And Ryke yearned to have some of her spirit himself. Just the sound of her voice made him ready to fight again, fed his confidence, reminded him of all those things a *luxa* was supposed to bring to an *umbro*.

Could all of the myth be true?

No, she was trying to seduce him into believing it. Weaving it into the story she wanted him to believe with a skill that took his breath away.

"Although," she mused. "It is kind of interesting to have you at my mercy like this." He felt her run a proprietary hand over him. Her caress was welcome, solace when he needed it most. He studied her and was relieved to see that her gaze was clear and confident again, those flames dancing in her eyes. She looked as if she would take on the universe and give it a good fight, as if she'd go down swinging—if she went down at all. Ryke wanted to really kiss her even as the display flickered on the far wall.

"Looks like we'll have company soon," Anguissa said and rose to her feet, snakes swaying, ready for another round. How many jumps had she endured in rapid succession? Ryke had to admire her stamina. He admired more than that as he watched her, hating that he was unable to stand alongside her. "Strength is where you find it, Ryke," Anguissa murmured. "You can choose to use the power you have."

It was true. The drug still held his body in thrall, but he wasn't completely helpless.

He had his mind.

He had his skill.

He could accept her invitation. It would be a feint, because she'd believe they were allied, but neither of them would survive alone.

It was the best of an array of bad choices.

Now that he was warned of her powers, surely he could protect himself against them?

He was never going to see his son again otherwise.

Anguissa didn't glance back, but as she strode forward to face the display, Ryke slipped.

Welcome back she thought, her tone amused but unsurprised. *What's a* custo?

The one who watches over me while I slip.

More than a servant.

More than a friend. It's a bond from birth.

But Bakiel's asleep now.

That's not the only rule I'm breaking with you, Princess.

There was exasperation in her tone when she replied. *And you think it was unpredictable for you to come back for Bakiel? Oh, Ryke. If you continue to be so honorable, you might end up being my HeartKeeper, after all.*

Ryke felt panic slide through him. *There's no such thing as love, Snake-Eyes.*

Oh good, I'm safe then.

Was she mocking him? Without seeing her expression, Ryke couldn't be sure.

You felt a bit worried there for a moment, Ryke. Is love that terrifying a possibility?

It's a fiction, but sharing thoughts with someone who believes nonsense poses definite risks.

Anguissa chuckled under her breath. *Her Starpod is in the hold. You can slip into her and make her return to it. Then we eject her, seize control of the freighter, and abandon her in this quadrant.*

Ryke was dismissive of the suggestion. *It doesn't work like that. I can only compel the host to do what he or she already wants to do. There has to be some urge and Hellemut won't leave this freighter.*

All right then. She needs some motivation.

Good luck motivating her to do anything she doesn't already want to do.

Oh, Ryke, you're being defeatist.

Realist, Princess.

Let's make a little bet.

This is serious...

It is. If I get her into the Starpod, I win.

Win what, Snake-Eyes?

Anguissa ignored his question and Ryke figured he could guess the answer. If she won, it wouldn't be much of a loss on his part. She had a plan, and he was curious as to what it might be. He tried to investigate her mind, but she had him confined in a specific area, trapped where he could only see her present observations. Her past and her memories were like sealed vaults.

She shouldn't have been able to to do that.

She should have been an open book to him.

He wasn't surprised, not anymore, but he knew he

should have been a lot more worried than he was.

It wasn't a surprise that Anguissa wouldn't follow anybody's rules.

The communications screen snapped to life, displaying Captain Hellemut on the deck. She leered at them and Ryke was glad he was immobilized.

He wouldn't have been able to hide his revulsion and that wouldn't have helped them one bit.

Hellemut was already going to be vengeful, given that he'd refused to help her doppelganger survive.

When Anguissa had first ventured away from Incendium, she'd been surprised to discover how many sentient life forms in the universe were bipeds. She supposed that symmetry made for elegant design, and that having two of most body parts was the most efficient way of guarding against debilitating injuries. There were exceptions, though, and she could never become accustomed to tripeds.

She'd heard in space bars that tripeds could be doubly or even triply endowed, with a set of genitals at each junction, but Anguissa had never seen one naked. She didn't want to. There was something about tripeds that disgusted her and she had a hard time keeping her expression impassive as she approached the display of Captain Hellemut.

Tripeds could travel at amazing speeds, but the coordination of their limbs while running required a higher level of fitness. In Anguissa's experience, as tripeds aged, they either concentrated on their physical welfare, or they abandoned all pretense of remaining agile and became sedentary.

Captain Hellemut was of the latter variety. She was monstrously large, with skin of a deep yellow hue, and her green eyes seemed to be half buried in her face. Her malice was clear, though, and not to be under-estimated.

They were alive still, which meant they were useful.

Or valuable.

Why?

Anguissa had to think that her own survival was due to Hellemut's desire to claim the Archangel.

Which had to be about that cargo.

How much did Ryke know about the Gloria Furore and their plans?

It was time to find that out. Anguissa sought a memory, then pulled it to the fore of her thoughts before she could reconsider the urge to trust an *umbro* who was already in her mind.

Can you read this, Ryke?

She felt him recoil. It was the warning label on the most carefully packed item in that bootleg cargo and the one that had fascinated Anguissa. The container itself was of the kind used for biohazards, and its presence was the reason she'd quarantined the hold of the Archangel.

His reaction spoke volumes, but Anguissa wanted more.

Can you?

Where did you see that, Snake-Eyes?

It's in the hold of the Archangel.

Then you did look!

Of course, I looked. I'm not going to haul garbage across the galaxy, given the price of fuel these days.

Ryke sighed. *Then the stories are true.* Before Anguissa could ask, he continued. *There have been rumors of a virus being bred in the illicit labs of Gungalorus, engineered to affect all carbon-based life forms. A custom job.*

I can guess the client.

You'd guess right. There are also rumors that it was stolen by the lead bio-chemist, now dead. Hellemut received coded messages about it after your first appearance near the Armada Seven.

And you broke the code.

Call it a hobby.

The Gloria Furore could hold any system hostage over the threat of releasing such a virus upon their populace. They'd paid for its creation and it had been stolen. Of course, they'd want it back.

Hellemut might want it badly enough to let Anguissa live for a while longer.

Would it be long enough?

After? So, that's not why Bond planted the worm?

No, it wasn't. Wait. You've decided Bond was the culprit?

Don't gloat, Ryke, just because you were right. She heard him chuckle. *Is it a deadly virus?*

What other kind would matter?

Excellent. Now we have something to bargain with.

Snake-Eyes....

Quiet, Ryke. I'm going to steal this freighter and it isn't going to be easy. Helpful comments only, please. This isn't a good time for me to fail.

"You will understand, Princess Anguissa, that I am reluctant to invite you to the deck to parlay, given your destructiveness in the Armada Seven," Hellemut said.

"I suppose you can't be too cautious," Anguissa replied. "Although insulting me when I control everything you desire might be seen as a diplomatic mistake."

"Everything I desire? Surely you exaggerate."

Anguissa just smiled.

Hellemut's sobered. "And what cause have you for insult?"

"Being attacked. Being locked in the chart room with a known traitor."

"You did destroy the nav system of the Armada Seven, condemning that crew."

Anguissa waved a hand, pretending to care less than she did. "Minions aren't worthy of my concern." She didn't feel badly that there were fewer members of the Gloria Furore using oxygen, although she felt badly for those in the crew who'd been enslaved. On the other hand, death might have been a relief, compared to serving under Hellemut's command.

"And my survival?"

"That wasn't you. It was one of your doppelgangers." Anguissa leaned closer. "You might be one of Hellemut's doppelgangers. I'm not convinced that the real Captain Hellemut would risk her survival by boarding this freighter."

Hellemut smirked. "Where is the risk? This freighter is under the complete control of the Gloria Furore. We set a trap for Ryke and he took the bait."

"Why?"

"I never trust an *umbro*. He might not have slipped during his torture, but that was only because his *custo* wasn't with him."

"I thought *umbros* were myths," Anguissa replied but Hellemut shook her head.

"They're very useful spies. We like to convince all of them who cross our paths to join our ranks. Ryke was, unfortunately, resistant to such persuasion. It would have been so much easier for him to capitulate."

Anguissa already knew that surrender wasn't in Ryke's vocabulary. "And yet I felt strangely compelled to destroy the Armada Seven as soon as I arrived on the transport deck and then to flee with Ryke. I think he must have slipped and used me for his own nefarious purposes."

Nefarious, Ryke echoed.

Anguissa ignored him.

Hellemut's eyes narrowed. "An *umbro* can only influence a victim to follow his or her own secret desires."

"Is it so unlikely that I'd want to survive?" Anguissa asked. "Once the nav system and deck of the Armada Seven was destroyed, everyone aboard was condemned."

Hellemut regarded her for a long moment, obviously

considering this argument. "Don't insult my intelligence by insisting that Ryke slipped into you on the Armada Seven, or suggest that you're a victim," she said softly, but Anguissa could see that she was already wondering.

"And don't insult mine by insisting that I would board a vessel, destroy its systems, and leave myself with no means of survival, other than relying upon some member of the enemy crew to save me." Her snakes were thrashing in anger and Anguissa knew that Hellemut was giving credence to her charge. "Someone put a worm in the Archangel's nav system before it left the first confrontation with the Armada Seven, a worm that would ensure we met again. I don't think that was a coincidence."

"There are no coincidences, Princess Anguissa."

"My thinking exactly. Someone compelled me to damage the deck of the Armada Seven far beyond my plans. Why would I put myself in such peril? No, my argument was with you, because I didn't realize then that I'd been betrayed by someone on my own crew. I would have been content to kill your doppelganger, Captain Hellemut, and I don't make mistakes of that magnitude."

Hellemut chuckled. "Have you figured out who it was yet?"

Surprise is on your side here, Snake-Eyes. Ryke prompted and Anguissa knew he was right.

"Of course. What was Bond's price?"

Hellemut scoffed. "The predictable one. Greed." She yawned. "He's been well compensated for his years of spying for the Gloria Furore."

Anguissa swallowed her anger, knowing that she'd deal with Bond later. She gestured to Ryke, still limp in his seat behind her. "What's the punishment for treason? More fire ants?"

Hellemut laughed.

"Usually it would be something like that, but things

have changed. A bounty has been offered for Ryke since his flight from the Armada Seven, a reward for him dead or alive," she provided, her voice crackling a bit through the comm. "With a bonus for delivering him dead."

Anguissa frowned. "That makes no sense," she said to Hellemut. "If I wanted someone dead, I'd pay extra for the satisfaction of doing it myself."

Good to know, Princess.

"I don't argue the terms." Hellemut's voice dropped lower. "You appear to be concerned for the fate of your companion, Princess Anguissa. Would you care to negotiate for his survival?"

"No, I was just curious." Anguissa was deliberately dismissive. "I'd rather negotiate for mine, thanks, especially since he took advantage of me to try to create his own escape." She turned her back on Ryke again, well aware that he was simmering in her thoughts as he listened. "Unless he's worth more than the Archangel."

Hellemut's eyes narrowed. "The Archangel?"

"You said you want the Archangel, Captain Hellemut, presumably because you want to reclaim the virus in its hold commissioned by the Gloria Furore and stolen by its creator, a bio-chemist who died without revealing what he'd done with the prize. My ship, containing that virus, is in secure quarantine. Only I can release it."

Hellemut was startled to silence.

Bold play, Princess.

Wait for it, Ryke.

"I'm sure your DNA could be preserved, if you died, Princess Anguissa, and any code broken over time."

"Both reasonable assumptions, but my kind are particularly concerned about protecting our treasures. And I used my best defenses, since I intend to collect the reward for the virus myself. It's not a biologically-based lock."

Hellemut stared at her.

"But perhaps we could make a deal," Anguissa continued. "Your facilitation and my code to unlock the quarantine, in exchange for shared credit."

"What facilitation?"

"Let me out of this chart room. Away from this traitor." Anguissa took a step closer to the screen. "It would be much smarter to negotiate details face-to-face."

"Why should I trust you enough to let you on deck?"

"Because I'm Gloria Furore, too," Anguissa said with breezy confidence. She smiled at the astonished commander of the vessel. "We're on the same side, Captain Hellemut. How like our leaders to launch two volleys after the same target."

Hellemut blinked.

And Anguissa struggled not to wince as Ryke roared furiously in her mind.

Snake-Eyes!

It couldn't be true.

Anguissa couldn't be Gloria Furore.

But she was a space pirate, even if Ryke had believed her to be one inclined to lesser violence than his captors had been. She had no interest in rules and charted her own course. She said she'd been piloting payloads for over three hundred years, and Ryke knew that few survived in that trade for very long.

Never mind who would be invited to a black market auction like the one where she'd bought the stolen virus.

On the other hand, he knew better than to trust her. He had no intention of being seduced by beauty again.

It would have been prudent to withdraw from Anguissa's mind, but he wanted to know what Hellemut said to her. He wanted to know what Anguissa said and did, and he couldn't accomplish much in his body's drugged state. He hoped the risk was worth the reward.

Don't abandon me now. Anguissa's thought was firm. *I'll*

need help to get through the interrogation.

Because you're not really Gloria Furore?

Don't tell me that my feint was so good that even you fell for it?

Ryke would have smiled if it had been possible.

You're going to need three codes and a ritual handshake. Reach for her middle hand, touch your longest finger to the tip of hers, incline your head in a bow, and then shake her hand. Cross your left hand over your right and shake her left hand.

What about her right hand?

She'll put it over top of your crossed hands. Bow more deeply then.

Got it.

Speak first and say "Andromeda rising." She'll reply and your reply will be based on hers.

Sounds thin, Soul-Snatcher.

It's a stall for time while she verifies your credentials.

Then you'd better get busy forging them.

Anguissa had to be striding along the corridor toward the deck. Ryke was aware that she could smell the canteen and tried to estimate her moment of arrival. He could share her thoughts, but he didn't know everything Anguissa knew. He realized there had been limitations when he'd slipped before, but he hadn't been so aware of the host's boundaries as he was with Anguissa.

I need a little help, Ryke.

No kidding, Princess. You're going to need a lot of help to pull this off and it's not going to be easy to fake on any timeline. There are no files supporting your membership claim, no dossier on you...

She interrupted him. *But there has to be a secured storage area in the ship's electronic memory. It's going to take her time to get into those files and to be certain that there's no record of me joining the Gloria Furore.*

And?

You're a code jockey, Ryke, by your own admission. If you're half as good as you say you are, you'll falsify an infection alert, one that says I'm a carrier of the virus in the Archangel's hold, and you'll do it fast.

Have you forgotten that I'm sedated, Snake-Eyes?

Have you forgotten that you can slip, Ryke? Bakiel can be your fingers if you slip into his mind.

Ryke was outraged. *I can't slip into two minds at once and it's not smart for an* umbro *to slip into his* custo *anyway. Never mind that I'd have to abandon you to Hellemut...*

Anguissa's response was warm. *I knew you cared, Ryke. Get me through the handshake then tell me how to get Bakiel the access he needs.*

And then?

And then I'll think of something. I'll stall.

It's a long shot, Snake-Eyes.

Really? I assumed your confidence was earned, Ryke, since you call yourself the best. She paused for a heartbeat. *Bond could have done it, you know.*

The comment about Bond made Ryke want to spit, or better, show Anguissa who was the better man.

She knew how to provide motivation, that was for sure.

Your taste for danger could leave us both dead, Princess.

We're dead anyway, Ryke. The long shot is the only chance we've got.

As much as Ryke hated to admit it, she was right.

Could Ryke do it?

Anguissa seriously hoped so.

Hellemut's suspicion was a tangible force on the deck. Even the robot Piper Twelve seemed to exude skepticism. They didn't act against her, though, which meant they still weren't sure. The cross-check was in progress but not complete.

Anguissa sauntered onto the deck as if she owned it and surveyed her surroundings. *Where?* She thought the question for Ryke.

Comm station. Ryke supplied tersely. *It has the weakest*

security so the ship can be easily hailed by alien systems.

Anguissa performed the handshake with Hellemut, ensuring that she ended up near the comm station. "Andromeda rising," she said when the handshake was done.

"Quasar eclipsed," Hellemut replied softly.

Ryke chuckled in Anguissa's thoughts. He said something in a language she didn't speak and she repeated it carefully.

Hellemut's eyes glinted with either surprise or satisfaction, and she lounged in the captain's chair, studying Anguissa with much greater interest than before. "You are filled with hidden surprises, Princess Anguissa."

Anguissa sat down at the comm station, making it look as if she had chosen the nearest seat. "Aren't we all?" she replied easily. *What the fark was that about?*

You just revealed that you have a higher rank than she does. It'll make her cautious.

Brilliant, Ryke. Remind me to reward you for that stroke of genius.

Only if we get to celebrate our survival of certain death again.

Enough chit-chat. Get busy so we can do that.

Can you put your hand on the tracking pad and glance down without appearing to do so?

Of course.

Anguissa began to shift shape, but didn't let the shimmer of her dragon side eclipse her humanoid form. Her senses sharpened but she didn't even have a blue light around her form. It was a trick she'd learned by accident and perfected over the monotony of long jumps, because it was so useful. Her dragon had extremely keen vision and could make sense of large quantities of information with the barest look. She barely cast a glance at the display, but her dragon memorized every line, as well as the layout of the keyboard and station. She smiled at Hellemut as the information unfurled in her mind and she heard Ryke's inhalation of surprise.

"And so, Princess Anguissa, what do you want in exchange for the security code?"

"A reason to give it to you, Captain Hellemut," Anguissa said smoothly. "After all, I should follow orders and surrender it to my superior."

"But you're in a compromised situation." Hellemut smiled. "I don't have to release you."

"And see that virus lost forever? I don't think you would be so disloyal to our order, Captain Hellemut." Anguissa traced a lazy fingertip on the console. "It could be hazardous to your career."

Later, Snake-Eyes. Don't do anything I wouldn't do. Ryke's thoughts were crisp and he was gone before Anguissa had time to reply. Her mind felt lonely. Echoing with emptiness. She realized how easy it would be to become accustomed to sharing thoughts with him. She'd never had a real partner, never had that profound trust of another person, and she felt naked in Ryke's absence.

It was unsettling, both to miss him and to realize how quickly her dependence had grown. Was this what it was like to have a HeartKeeper? Would she ever know?

Anguissa strove to hide her reaction from Hellemut. She lifted her brows. "Unless you have retirement plans beyond the Gloria Furore?"

"Of course not. I could still steal the Archangel and force the hold open."

"The containment unit is of excellent design."

"I could attack and destroy the Archangel, and loose the virus on Incendium."

Anguissa had thought of that, many times, and she pretended to be more confident than she was. "Impossible. An armed vessel would never get close enough. You would be destroyed before there was any chance of fulfilling your plan." She shook her head and spoke slowly, hoping to give Ryke as much time as possible. There was only so far she could stretch this discussion. "It seems to be a plan that's unworthy of your intelligence, Captain Hellemut. No, you need me, even if you don't want to admit it."

"Do I?"

"Oh, yes. Luckily for you, I don't actually need the credit for delivering that payload. I'm willing to share."

Hellemut's eyes immediately narrowed. "Why?"

It was Anguissa's moment to prevaricate. She spun the chair then rose to her feet, strolling across the deck as if acquainting herself with its design. "I don't know that I need to reveal that detail."

"You do, if you expect me to trust you."

Anguissa laughed. "Trust? I didn't know we were talking about trust, Captain Hellemut. I thought we were talking about ensuring personal advantage."

"What benefit could you possibly see by letting me deliver the payload?"

Anguissa wagged her finger. "A clever question," she had time to say before the biohazard alarm sounded.

Thank fark for that.

Or maybe she should thank Mercado.

The distinctive whoop was a universal alarm, used on all vessels, legitimately registered or not. Hellemut paled, staring at Anguissa's cool smile. She spun in her chair and scrabbled at the closest console. "Report!" she barked, then fixed a glare upon Piper Twelve.

The robot had plugged his fingertip into a port on the closest comm. "Level seven biohazard detected on deck. Toxin is highly infectious, organic and threatening to one organism currently on deck. Evacuate. Evacuate."

"One organism?" Hellemut echoed.

Anguissa shrugged. "You can't catch a virus you already carry. Apparently, dragon shifters have a longer incubation period but the virus remains very infectious. Good to know, don't you think?"

"You! You brought the virus from the Archangel!" Hellemut fell backward, her hand over her mouth.

"I volunteered to test it," Anguissa lied. She saw Hellemut stagger, then straighten, purpose filling her features. "That's why I don't need credit for delivering it. I've got more credit with the Gloria Furore than I can use in this lifetime."

"You lied to me!" Hellemut cried and Anguissa laughed.

"While you're always honest? I don't think so, Hellemut."

Hellemut ran toward the portal, moving as quickly as she could.

"Don't go!" Anguissa said. "Not when the conversation is just getting interesting." Hellemut didn't stop, but Anguissa wanted to make sure she kept running. She summoned the change, feeling the fire charge through her body and reveling in its power. The shift was liberating, potent, and truly wonderful.

This time, she didn't attack the nav system. She did however exhale a long hot breath after the fleeing Hellemut. Anguissa recognized that Ryke had slipped into Hellemut by the change in her posture. Hellemut moved with Ryke's decisive purpose. The former captain didn't even bother to secure the door, as she strode toward the hold.

Ryke managed to propel her even more quickly than she would have gone herself.

Anguissa understood. Hellemut wanted to leave now, so Ryke could expedite her departure. And then what? Would Ryke feast on Hellemut? Devour her soul, the way *umbros* were rumored to do, and feed his own strength with that of another? Would he feast until Hellemut bled to death, alone in her Starpod? Could he refrain from doing what was his nature to do? Could he stop once it had started?

Anguissa shuddered, feeling that it had been foolish to let him into her own mind. It had been a question of survival—and she wouldn't do it again.

She turned off the display, not wanting to watch.

Piper Twelve was motionless, clearly uncertain of how to proceed. He hadn't been programmed for this situation. Anguissa recognized that Ryke had left the robot to her while he eliminated Hellemut.

"Release the docking mechanism and open the hold, Piper Twelve," she commanded.

The robot hesitated.

"I'm taking command of the Magnetawan, in the absence of any other authority."

"Yes, Captain Anguissa." He did as instructed, and they watched in silence as the Starpod left the ship and sailed into the void.

Had Hellemut lost her mind yet? From what distance could Ryke slip back to his own body? Anguissa didn't know. She feared then that he might not return and found that an unsettling possibility—even knowing what he was.

He was an unsettling man with a disconcerting effect upon her. Anguissa couldn't blame it on the scent of the Seed anymore.

Miss me, Snake-Eyes? Cocky, convinced of his own charm and sounding suspiciously more vigorous. He *had* feasted.

Even so, Anguissa was glad to hear his voice.

Nice timing, Ryke.

So you didn't miss me. His tone was wry, and Anguissa took a chance.

She provoked him by letting him see her horror of what he was.

Next time, I'll go for good. His thought was soft, almost a threat as well as a promise. Anguissa wished they could talk about it, but she sensed Ryke's resistance. He was the one isolating his thoughts now, hiding his impressions and feelings from her.

She might as well have been alone.

They were too different. Their kinds would never get along. They'd survived Hellemut and that was the only common ground they'd ever had.

She wouldn't think about their child.

Anguissa pivoted to survey Piper Twelve. "I hate robots," she told him and thought she saw a flicker of trepidation even in his impassive expression.

Tell him to plug into the infinity port, Captain. Ryke was terse and Anguissa felt his tone like a slap. His nature wasn't his fault, she knew that, but she couldn't make peace with his need to feed.

The sooner he got to Centurios and their ways parted forever, the better.

"Plug into the infinity port, Piper Twelve." The robot hesitated and Anguissa filled her lungs with air, more than ready to fry him to cinders. "That would be a direct order, Piper Twelve." Her snakes were rising like cobras prepared to strike and when they hissed, he moved to do as instructed.

"What comes after, Captain Anguissa?"

Anguissa was so surprised by the question that she assumed she'd misunderstood. "What do you mean, Piper Twelve?"

"Is there chaos or oblivion after existence?"

Anguissa supposed a religious argument wouldn't be very compelling. She expected Ryke's commentary and missed it. "Personally, I'm hoping for oblivion."

"As am I." He plugged his finger into the portal and nothing happened for a moment. Then he jerked and began to make a whirring sound that couldn't have been one of his usual reactions. He looked toward Anguissa, as if to beg for mercy, and she breathed a targeted plume of fire, granting him the oblivion he desired.

When she was done, there was only a pile of blackened metal and wire remaining. She shifted back to her usual form and swept it into the grinder and disposal unit. She breathed a sigh of relief.

Ryke was silent.

Gone from her mind for good.

He'd done what he said he would do.

Anguissa knew she should be glad, but she did miss him. The upside of him abandoning her now was that her reliance upon him couldn't become worse. He wouldn't be able to destroy her, or their child. She'd take him home, wave goodbye, then go after Bond and the Archangel alone.

Too bad she couldn't summon much enthusiasm for her own vision of her future.

"Prepare to jump, gentlemen," she said into the comm, but no one replied.

Hellemut's mind was not a place where Ryke wanted to linger. He stayed only long enough to get her into her Starpod, then ensure it was locked and released from the dock. He programmed the nav and locked in the coordinates of a distant destination, one that she had insufficient fuel to reach.

Would it be a lack of fuel or oxygen that ensured her demise? Ryke didn't care. She was doomed, which evened the score.

When there was no chance of Hellemut turning back, he abandoned her to her fate. He slipped into Anguissa's mind, triumphant, only to be shocked by her horror of what he was.

She thought he was feasting upon Hellemut's *anima*.

She was revolted by the idea. The power of her emotional reaction shook Ryke to his core. How could she so despise what he was? How could she blame him for his own nature? How could she have shared his thoughts and not realized that he was different from his fellows, by choice?

Once, Ryke would have slipped away, but Anguissa said she was carrying his son. He owed that child the opportunity to know his or her own father. This might be his last chance to leave a legacy of any kind for his child. Anguissa couldn't go to Centurios and survive, but the presence of his son there meant that Ryke didn't want to be anywhere else.

Anguissa announced the impending jump and Ryke knew he would dream of a failure. He was tempted to withdraw from her, but reconsidered.

Could he choose his dream and show Anguissa something specific from his past? Could he give her a story to share with their child, the child he would never see?

Ryke was certainly going to try.

CHAPTER SEVEN

Anguissa dreamed of blood. Copious quantities of it, running in the streets of a city she didn't recognize. She could smell it, she could feel it slipping beneath her boots, she could taste the tang of it in the air. It was metallic, distinctive, yet in this dream, it was more.

It was life.

She was aware of the power in the blood, the elusive ether that animated all beings, that made them more than the sum of their biological parts. Her lust to consume blood was so strong that she knew it couldn't be her own. She hated the smell of blood herself, but in this dream, it awakened a desire within her that was both powerful and unfamiliar.

An *umbro's* thirst for blood.

She was sharing Ryke's dream again.

Anguissa was curious despite herself. What would this memory tell her about him?

This city must be on Centurios. This battle must have been important. He was at the fore of a battalion of troops, armored, and each fighting with two blades. The other army were feasting upon the dead and were apparently dizzy with the power of the blood. They'd been distracted from the fight by the satisfaction of their base desire. Anguissa felt his disgust for his opponents.

But weren't they the same kind? Weren't they all *umbros?*

Ryke's troops cut through the ranks of the feasting army, dealing death with merciless efficiency. She felt how the scent of blood fed a ruthlessness deep inside Ryke, how it summoned a ferocity that she associated with *umbros.*

She also felt Ryke's own abhorrence of his body's desires, yet his inability to be anything other than he was. When the battle was over and the street strewn with bodies, his men feasted in their turn.

But they didn't drink blood. They inhaled the escaping spirits of the dead warriors. Through Ryke's eyes, Anguissa could see the life spirits rising, like mist over the bodies that could not longer serve their will.

Ryke bent over a dying warrior, looking into his eyes, seeing his acceptance that he would never hunt again. As Ryke watched, the light in the warrior's eyes was extinguished. A fine mist rose from him, a mist in rainbow hues, and Ryke breathed deeply, inhaling it all.

Anguissa felt its power surge through Ryke's body, adding strength to his own. She felt the dead warrior's virility and power redouble Ryke's own, making him more than he had been before.

The startling thing to Anguissa was that the feasting prompted a similar rush within Ryke as shifting shape did within her. She understood that he was doing what he had been born to do, that he was following the impulse of his kind, and that his very nature rewarded that.

Could she blame him for being what he was?

Could she despise him for being good at what he was?

As she wondered, Ryke straightened and looked over the battlefield after he had feasted, considering the fallen in the streets of the city, and she felt his heart clench with disapproval. She felt the loathing within him, the disgust with his nature that was so similar to her own reaction.

And when a subordinate soldier beckoned him to the side of the leader of the opposing forces, a powerful warrior on the cusp of death with blood on his mouth, Ryke turned away.

"No more," he said with resolve. "I have feasted to sustain myself, and will feast no more."

"But..." the subordinate protested, clearly confused.

"He is yours," Ryke said. "A reward for valor this day."

Confusion lit the other subordinate's gaze but then the other warrior breathed his last. At the sight of the rising spirit, again a rainbow-hued mist, the hunger claimed him. Ryke watched him feast, noting that he was insatiable, well aware that the craving was the weakness of his kind.

They could be betrayed by their own desires, just as this opposing battalion had felt compelled to stop and feast before the battle was won. They were more primitive than Ryke's kind, feasting on blood instead of spirit, but they were *umbros*, too, and Anguissa felt Ryke's determination to never be driven by his own base need.

He vowed to rise above it, which meant he would eliminate its power. He would achieve that the same way he accomplished all of his goals, with discipline and resolve, with training and denial, and his body would slowly learn to find sustenance elsewhere.

Anguissa felt his conviction and admired it. Could she have denied her own nature, even if she had desired to do so?

The stream of memories flowed more quickly then, and she had the sense that Ryke was deliberately revealing his truth to her. She certainly was learning more about him than she had in the past. She watched him train himself to survive without feasting. She saw him turn away from temptation, time and again. She saw him find satisfaction of a much lesser kind in the exchange of ideas, in the sparkle of conversation, in the tingle of sexual tension. It was like subsisting on appetizers instead of banquets, but Ryke exercised vigorously to keep his hunger tamed. She was in awe of his conviction and his discipline.

Was this why his father had wanted him dead?

She viewed the memory of Ryke's capture by the Gloria Furore and felt his love for his son in those last moments they shared together. She was certain then that he was curating memories for her and she couldn't help but be flattered by that. He skimmed through the interrogation by the Gloria Furore, the refusal of Centurios to ransom him, the profound relief he felt when he learned that his son had been returned home.

They tried to tempt him to show his ability as an *umbro*, to do what he couldn't resist doing. They exposed him to blood, to dying warriors, to the bodies of those who didn't survive interrogation. Ryke held fast, and it was likely only possible because of his own earlier training, his own decision. They taunted him with the spirits of warriors of ill repute and those of uncommon valor. They teased him with possibilities, but Ryke refused to feast. They isolated him from conversation and contact with any sentient beings, but he dug into his determination and did not feast, even when a morsel was offered to him in his starvation.

Could Anguissa have been as persistent?

She lived through the horror of the immersion in fire ants, the excruciating pain of the millions of simultaneous bites. She shared his disgust of them climbing toward his mouth and nose, and the terror that they would suffocate him. The fear didn't lessen at all with each successive bath, but Ryke did not break.

And she felt the change manifest within him during the last immersion. His skin was aching and raw from the bites. It burned with pain that was only multiplied when the ants began to gnaw upon him again. His fists clenched and his body went taut as the tide of ants rose over his knees, over his hips, over his chest, then the worst possible thing happened: the fire ants climbed over his chin, over his lips. He kept his mouth clenched shut, but they charged into his nostrils. He gagged and his lips parted, and they surged forth like a tide, flowing into his mouth and down his throat.

Ryke roared in horror, convinced that he would die of the biting invasion.

Suddenly, a tide of fire swept through him. He felt as if he was lit from within, as if a flame had taken up residence in his veins. He had been briefly convinced that he was dying, that the torment would end, but then a wave of well-being suffused him.

He had changed.

Ryke felt so potent that he might have been immortal, but he hid his reaction from his captors. He sagged in his bonds and was lifted from the vat. The fire ants retreated, flowing from his every orifice, leaving him transformed from within.

He had been reforged. Ryke didn't know why or how, and neither did Anguissa. The feeling faded, just as surely as his appetite for spirit and even blood faded. He almost yearned to be dipped in the vat of fire ants again, in the hope that he might escape. Instead, the Gloria Furore tired of him and his resistance and assigned him to the Armada Seven.

He was no longer what he had been, but his transformation to something new was incomplete.

They came out of the jump and Anguissa stared at the display of the deck, her assumptions shaken by all that Ryke had shared.

Was it possible for anyone to change their fundamental nature? Anguissa would have said no, but after the memories Ryke had shared, she was no longer certain.

If anyone could do it, it would require the kind of resolve he'd shown.

Was it possible that she felt admiration for an *umbro*?

"In the beginning, there was the *anima*," Bakiel said softly. Anguissa turned from her position in the captain's chair to find the *custo* just inside the door from the lower deck. He looked even less substantial than he had previously, as pale as a morning mist and just as ethereal.

"The spirit?"

"The essence that feeds all living things. Some call it the soul. Some call it the essence. On Centurios, we have always called it the *anima*." He nodded and stepped onto the deck at Anguissa's gesture of invitation. "It filled all living things, giving them purpose and power, coursing through their blood, firing their thoughts, driving their bodies. And as the origin of all life, it became a commodity of value."

He sat before her, glancing at the display of the stars. They might as well have been alone in this sector of this quadrant, all other vessels far away. They were cruising toward Centurios.

"Where's Ryke?"

"He sleeps. Between the sedative's effects and the exertion, never mind the trials of his servitude, he is exhausted."

Anguissa frowned, knowing she needed to ask the question but already guessing the answer. She had to be sure. "But he slipped into Hellemut. He possessed her *anima* and drove her to her death. Didn't he feast?"

Bakiel shook his head. "No, he swore to abandon the habits of his kind many, many years ago. His word is his bond, regardless of the cost to himself."

"He smells like an *umbro*."

Bakiel considered this. "He was born an *umbro*. He chooses to be both more and less than that."

"You don't need to watch over him? I thought that was what a *custo* did."

"I watch over him when he slips, not when he sleeps," Bakiel corrected. "And I serve him in all ways. You need to know his history and so I will tell you what Ryke will not."

"What's a *luxa*?"

Bakiel smiled. "The light in the darkness, of course. The beacon in the night. His destined mate, the one who will make him complete so that he can fulfill the prophecy of our kind."

Anguissa's heart skipped. "Funny he didn't mention that."

"Ryke has never believed in prophecies. His caste tend not to. They discard them and forget them, but we *custos* preserve all such details. It is part of our service."

"Tell me about Centurios."

"Is that a personal device?" he asked instead, indicating the film applied to her arm.

Anguissa nodded. "I think the energy beams on the Armada Seven destroyed its power source."

"Let me see it."

"You do repairs as well as cook?"

Bakiel smiled. "I serve. It is my place and the source of my satisfaction." He beckoned and Anguissa removed the film, liking the care he showed when examining it. He laid it flat on a console, then searched for tools and parts. The design allowed for easy substitutions, Anguissa knew that, but she didn't have the skill to do more than basic repairs herself.

As he worked, Bakiel talked, his voice a low litany. "On Centurios, the *anima* was believed to reside in the blood. A race evolved that could feast directly upon the blood. In time, their hunger and their numbers grew so that they were feared by the others of our world. They were always a minority, but their feasting gave them power over others."

"I can understand that."

"Initially, they were indistinguishable from us, but they became hunted for a time. Their days in darkness, hiding from persecution, changed them, made them darker, made them seem less substantial."

"*Umbros.*"

"*Umbros,*" Bakiel agreed. "Once they took to the shadows, more than their appearance changed. They dreamed of the life they had enjoyed before being compelled to hide and yearned to restore it. That could only occur if they were in command, and the scheming began to make that so. They built their numbers, they rose in darkness, and they claimed the royal palace by force. For centuries they ruled, and so long as their blood toll was filled, they were reasonable rulers."

"The blood toll must have ensured that they were hated, though."

"Not so long as we waged war and they consumed those we conquered. But in time, the armies led by *umbros* conquered all of the other cities on Centurios, bringing all under their dominion. In comparative peace, there were fewer to feast upon. Unbeknownst to those outside their kind, some of the *umbros* were changing. They remained predators and still sought the *anima*, but they had evolved to find it without feasting upon the blood."

Anguissa thought of Ryke's vision in the dream, of the fine mist rising from those recently deceased. That must have been the *anima.*

"*Umbros* had always been persuasive and had always possessed a kind of cunning that led victims closer to them. Some called it the ability to cast thoughts into other minds. They learned, from a combination of conquests and experimentation, to slip fully into the mind of a host organism and possess it."

"Then steal the *anima* and abandon the host to die."

"You disapprove." His tone was matter-of-fact, even as he deftly repaired the device. "The universe abounds with predators of one kind or another."

"But that's hunting of the most barbaric kind."

"Worse than drinking blood? Those victims didn't survive, either." He spared her a glance. "What of the victims of your dragon fire?"

The question reminded Anguissa of her sense during Ryke's dream that they had so much in common. "Stealing a soul seems worse."

"You're not alone in that view, Princess Anguissa. In fact, there was dissent within the ranks of the *umbros* themselves, until the new breed seized power in violent coup. They vowed to end the blood toll, so the people of Centurios supported them. But after the final battle, they feasted upon the *anima* of the defeated *umbros* for ten days and nights. Once the *animae* of the defeated *umbros* had been consumed, companies of soldiers took to the streets, seizing the *animae* of citizens. Chaos ruled. It is said that darkness fell completely upon Centurios with that victory."

"A figure of speech?"

"A truth. The capital city turned from the sun and the planet's rotation slowed so that the city remains in perpetual twilight. The citizens live in terror and leave their homes as infrequently as possible. It is said that the hunger of the *umbros* is so great that they can influence the sun, the moon, and the stars."

Anguissa raised her brows but didn't comment.

"That they could change the rotation of the planet convinced many that they are sorcerers as well as predators."

Anguissa remembered the shadows in the arena, the flickering fires around the perimeter of its central ring.

"That fear would minimize the chance of rebellion."

"It has."

"And what about *custos*? Where do you come in?

"We always served the *umbros*. It was our place. But once they began to hunt the *anima*, they needed greater protection and our role grew in importance."

"You stand guard over their bodies when they hunt."

"More than that, Princess Anguissa. We guard their stories and their secrets, as well as caring for their physical form. Ours is a bond of great trust." He began to put Anguissa's device back together, his fingers nimble.

"The fear of *umbros* is universal, even beyond Centurios."

"And for good reason. They are merciless predators."

"Yet you serve one."

"I had no choice, Princess Anguissa. I was born to be what I am." Bakiel frowned. "Have you ever seen an *umbro* feast?"

Anguissa shook her head, though she was thinking of Ryke's dream. "Not exactly."

"It is terrifying to witness. The *umbro* slips into the mind of the host and devours the *anima*, turning the host into a creature commanded by the *umbro*. All entities fight this invasion to a greater or lesser degree. Nature has an abhorrence of it, and it is uncommon for the situation to last long."

"The host dies," Anguissa guessed.

"The host's physical shell cannot sustain the *anima* of the *umbro*, not once it has devoured the host's own *anima*. There is too much spirit, too much essence, and the faults in the shell break. It is not uncommon for blood vessels to burst and barriers to be compromised. Once begun, the destruction can't be halted and such wholesale damage is nearly impossible to repair."

"But the *umbro* has the *anima*."

"And that is all the *umbro* wants. In times of war, the *umbros* can consume the departing *animae* from the dead, but when Centurios is at peace, the living become prey, just as they were all those years ago when their blood was sought by earlier *umbros*." He worked quietly for a few moments. "It's not a unique impulse to feast upon others. On other worlds, conquerors eat the hearts of those they defeat, wanting to take on the opponent's valor. Triumphant warriors eat the brains of their foes, or other organs, wanting to build their own powers after victory. They all seek the *anima*, but only the *umbros* refined the means of seizing it. And so, on Centurios, a planet ruled by *umbros* with no moral code and no mercy, a society where one is born into a caste and remains there until death, a civilization that seems sometimes to exist purely to feed the appetites of its rulers for more *animae*, a prophecy was born."

"That one day the *umbros* would fall from power?" Anguissa guessed.

Bakiel shook his head. "Change has to come from within when a society is ruled with such force."

"Or by invasion."

"No one would invade Centurios. The Gloria Furore hunt at the perimeter, wanting individual *umbros* for their own dark purposes, like predators claiming the isolated and the weak, but they have no desire to rule the planet. Centurios has weakened, for many will not trade with us, and many turn away our freighters for fear that they, too, will be invaded by *umbros*. Life is not good for those outside the imperial palace. Some even choose to be taken by *umbros*, to end their own misery."

Anguissa found that even more repulsive than Ryke's original nature. She was outraged that any ruler would keep citizens not only at disadvantage but in despair. "What was the prophecy, then?"

"That one day, there would be an *umbro* who would

change Centurios, an *umbro* with a moral code, an *umbro* who outlawed the act of feeding upon the living, one who would seek and provide justice for all. And this *umbro* would be recognized because he would find his *luxa*, and they would rule together for a thousand Centurios years over an era of prosperity and goodwill."

"A tempting prospect," Anguissa said, remembering Ryke's determination to save Bakiel. That had been the first hint that he was different from her expectation of *umbros*.

Bakiel nodded, his gaze fixed upon the device he repaired. "I was born to the lowest caste on Centurios, a caste devoted to the service of the *umbros*. We are assigned young to a specific *umbro* and sworn to serve him in all ways until our death. Many *umbros* feed upon the *anima* of their *custo*, when they haven't feasted. It is their right to take what they desire, to choose. It is our place to surrender whatever is demanded of us by our *umbros*, without protest or delay."

Anguissa was horrified by this situation. "And there's no reprieve?"

"Death, at which time the *umbro* has the right to claim the remains of the *custo's anima*."

"It sounds hopeless."

Bakiel nodded. "Unless, of course, one's *umbro* shows signs of fulfilling the prophecy we hold so dear. It was after the battle for the imperial throne that Ryke changed. The fight for supremacy was between bands of *umbros* because the emperor had died with no sons. Some followed a man who'd chosen the emperor's daughter, and others, led by Ryke's father, staged a coup. The fighting was savage. The streets ran with blood as *umbros* skipped from host to host, undermining the supporting forces of their opponents and building the power of their own *anima*. Soon, there were few left alive in the capital city. There was no regard for the survival of the other castes. In the end, more than two thirds of the city was dead or dying and terror filled the hearts of those who survived. Ryke's father crowned himself emperor and feasted slowly upon the *animae* of those he had defeated, as was tradition. Ryke declined to feast. He went into the streets and helped the other castes. It is rumored that he even shared of his *anima* and that he saved lives."

"Did he?"

Bakiel gave her a steady look. "It is not my place to tell you all. But on that day, Ryke vowed never to slip again. I know this because we argued about it."

"Doesn't his nature require him to feed?"

"His *anima* was strong, but his will was stronger. I believed it could not be done, and feared we would lose the one *umbro* with promise." Bakiel shrugged. "But he was adamant and he trained hard. For a time, I thought he might evade repercussions for his father seemed indulgent, but after Ryke had a son and the boy turned five, matters changed. Ryke was accused of treason by several senators for refusing to join the feast seven years before and for defying custom by aiding the other castes."

"And the punishment was to fight a hydra in the arena."

"It was said that his father defended his son privately, that he ensured Ryke faced a beast that could have been readily defeated. It was said that his father outlawed him only with great regret, because to not do as much would have cost him the imperial throne."

"Rumors," Anguissa scoffed.

"Rumors," Bakiel agreed easily, so easily that she knew he shared her doubts. "And so the only thing of value to Ryke was taken from him."

"Access to his son."

"He was provoked into abducting the boy. Everyone knew he would do it. I thought it was too easy to steal the Starpod, but all know I have a suspicious mind when it comes to enemies of my *umbro*."

"And your loyalty is returned," Anguissa noted with a smile.

Bakiel nodded. "He didn't have to return to the Magnetawan for me, but I knew he would."

"You believe that Ryke will fulfill the prophecy."

"He is an *umbro* of honor. He has found his *luxa*." Bakiel raised those pale eyes to meet Anguissa's gaze. "Now all he has to do is persuade her to return home with him—to step into the fire, so to speak—so that a new day may dawn on Centurios." He bowed slightly and returned the personal device to her.

Anguissa checked and found that it was functioning perfectly again. She smoothed it onto her inner arm, smiling with pleasure. "Thank you, Bakiel! Are you giving Ryke a lot of water?"

"Yes. The sedative will be flushed out of him as soon as possible."

"Good. Maybe this short jump will be easier for him than for us." She glanced to the *custo* who nodded. "Prepare to jump."

Mareeqa.

It had to be Mareeqa.

Ryke tried to evade the dream but it was unshakeable. He'd exerted himself so much to show Anguissa what he wanted his child to know about him, that he was tired and the dream of Mareeqa had hold of his thoughts before he could stop it.

Betrayed by beauty, one more time.

In his mind's eye, Ryke was striding toward the rental room, details of his scheduled breeding clear in his thoughts. He knew his partner had been chosen for the anticipated way her genetics would pair with his. Their offspring would carry the strengths of both partners. It would be a boy.

There was no romance about it. Every detail was calculated for maximum effect. The only concession to popular superstition was that the child would be delivered—or labor would be induced—on the prophesied day for the grandson of the new emperor to be born.

Ryke had declined the option of laboratory insemination. He wanted there to be no doubt that the child was his own. He had chosen instead for his selected mate to be quarantined with him for the entire period of her fertility.

They would have three days and nights of sex.

He would never see the mother of his son again after the birth. Her compensation was already deposited and would be released to her after the delivery of the healthy baby boy.

Ryke would have a son.

He had been chaste for two weeks to prepare. He was accompanied only by Bakiel on the day in question, as the plan for the conception was known to only a few.

The hotel was a sumptuous one, with every pleasure available. Ryke was greeted discreetly in the lobby and quickly ushered to the reserved suite. There was a certain ceremony about it all, and Ryke wondered if their mating would be observed. He was informed that Mareeqa had already arrived, left Bakiel outside the door of the suite, then opened the door.

Bakiel would stand watch. There were no other doors or accessible windows. Meals would be delivered by dumbwaiter, through a passageway too small for any intruder.

The child would be his, beyond doubt.

His heart skipped when the lock clicked behind him and his anticipation rose.

Ryke knew Mareeqa would be submissive, because all

women on Centurios knew their place. He was prepared for her to be pretty, as that would be superior genetically. He was certain she would be a princess, because that caste would be a suitable match for his own.

He opened the door to the suite and she was standing there, waiting for him, hands folded before herself and head bowed.

Ryke was astonished both that she was so beautiful and that his body responded to his first glimpse of her with such enthusiasm. Her hair was long and fair, curving over her shoulders and curling slightly at the ends. Her eyes were green and thickly lashed, tipping up slightly at the outer corners. Her lips were full and red, ripe for his kiss. Her curves were more than satisfactory and she was just a little shorter than him.

Delicate. Feminine. Demure.

Perfect.

She was a princess, so soft that her only function in life could be to offer pleasure to a man like Ryke. The way she cast down her lashes sent fire through him. She was almost naked, wearing just a sheer slip of a dress, as if she was dressed in mist and nothing more.

She was his to take.

And he would take her immediately.

Because all women on Centurios knew their place.

Anguissa wanted to scoff aloud. She hoped desperately that Mareeqa would prove to have some intellect or spirit to contribute to the union, but was pretty sure she'd be disappointed. This princess had no spark, no spirit, no opinion and no ideas of her own.

Delicate. Feminine. Demure.

Perfect.

Anguissa couldn't think of a more boring combination.

Mareeqa succumbed to Ryke's kiss immediately,

capitulating to him as if there was no other option. When he carried her to the couch in the suite, she lay exactly where he placed her, submissive.

Passive.

Anguissa saw that she had even lubricated herself in advance of Ryke's arrival, to add to his pleasure. She couldn't bear to watch the woman, who didn't appear even to be present for the ritual. She might have been having her nails buffed for all the interest she showed in having Ryke make love to her.

She was clearly an idiot.

Instead, Anguissa watched Ryke, which had been impossible during their own mating. He moved with the grace of a warrior and had all the power she remembered. He was a glorious sight in his nudity, all tanned masculine power. Anguissa wanted to lick him from head to toe— or tackle him herself. His muscles flexed as picked up Mareeqa, his hand slid up her thigh to caress her. Anguissa recalled his deft touch on the controls of the Starpod and the surety with which he had touched her.

Even though the Seed no longer called, she wanted Ryke again.

Maybe twice more.

She watched him ease himself into Mareeqa and was amazed that the woman seemed unaffected by his lovemaking. Anguissa could remember the thick hardness of him inside her, the way he had stretched her and filled her, her own hunger for more and more. Ryke gripped Mareeqa's buttocks and lifted her up, driving deeper inside her. She was as limp as a doll, her hands draped on his shoulders. Ryke kissed her, he claimed her, and he found his release with a triumphant shout.

Did he prefer women to be like this?

Anguissa was disappointed that Ryke's own thoughts were filled with satisfaction.

Mareeqa smiled slightly, running her fingers through

his hair as he rested atop her. Her impassivity would have infuriated Anguissa, but it seemed to incite Ryke's passion. She watched as he took her again, from behind, and again, in the bathing room, then again just before the dawn.

She wished she could turn off his memory. She had no ability to do that apparently—she tried—or to speed up the endless monotony of Ryke having sex with an inanimate object.

And loving it.

Finally, she couldn't keep quiet.

I thought you relived your failures in your dreams during jumps. I don't think anyone could criticize your performance here.

Jealous, Snake-Eyes?

No. I've never understood the appeal of pleasure androids.

Mareeqa wasn't an android.

She might as well have been. Did she ever have an orgasm? Is that what you see as a failure, that you couldn't make an android respond beyond her programming?

You are *jealous.* He seemed to find this amusing.

No, but you're far less than I thought, if this is passion worth remembering. I'm disappointed, Ryke. Only worthless men never take the risk of being out of control.

He was silent and she knew she'd found the root of it. Ryke wasn't nearly as confident as he liked her to believe.

I could turn that around, Princess. Maybe it's only worthless women who never take the risk of being out of control.

But I did take that risk. I let you be in charge, Ryke. Maybe you remember me asking you to claim me.

I remember. His words were low and pensive, sending a vibration through Anguissa that she wanted to explore.

It's a sign of trust, Ryke. How much do you trust me?

More than I should. Ryke's words were low enough to set Anguissa simmering again.

Good, because you still owe me for Hellemut.

They abruptly came out of the jump, just when she was enjoying herself, and Anguissa felt like junk. Ryke slipped out of her thoughts and she realized she was becoming accustomed to the intimacy of having him so close.

She missed him.

She admired him.

It was time to tell him so.

Why had he dreamed of Mareeqa? Ryke hadn't been able to think of anything else for those days in the suite, nothing beyond sex with Mareeqa, over and over again. He'd been consumed by his desire for her, yet while the memory provoked some reaction, the time with Mareeqa paled in recollection of being with Anguissa.

The display flickered to life on the opposite wall of the chart room. Anguissa looked tired but she smiled. The sight of her sent an increasingly familiar fire through Ryke.

He recalled the sense of being remade that he had in the vat of fire ants.

He recalled the feeling of being changed when he and Anguissa had first made love.

He avoided the conclusion Bakiel would have made, but still wanted to have one last union with Anguissa, before their ways parted forever.

He wanted to give her something to remember.

"Hello again and welcome to our final approach to the Centurios starport," Anguissa said. "We've just come out of the jump, but have a little cruise before we secure a docking location."

"I know where the wormhole comes out of deep space, Snake-Eyes. This is my home, remember."

"I do remember, Ryke. I also remember that all princesses on Centurios know their place. Think I'll be able to start an awakening?"

Bakiel chuckled, revealing that he was on the deck as well.

"Or maybe as an abomination, I won't have a chance." She leaned closer to the comm, her eyes dancing. "How's that sedative, Ryke?"

"Wearing off, thanks." Ryke rubbed his chin, feeling some growth of beard. Two jumps in rapid succession and his belly felt empty again. "Why?"

"Because I won our bet, Ryke, and I'm in command of this vessel. I'm thinking of giving you a direct order."

Ryke smiled, knowing exactly what that order would be. "I'm feeling particularly obedient, Snake-Eyes. Don't miss your chance."

Ryke made it to the captain's quarters just before Anguissa and paused to watch her approach. He loved the grace and power of her walk, that she was forthright and resolute. She was unlike any woman he'd ever known and he was surprised to realize that he liked that just fine.

In a way, it was too bad that they had no future together.

He wanted to see their child and was saddened that he never would.

Anguissa halted a few steps away from him, her snakes swaying, her dark eyes filled with mysteries as she studied him. "Tell me why you didn't feast on Hellemut."

"You are what you eat," he acknowledged.

"I'm serious." She came into the room and closed the door behind herself, sealing them into the space together. It immediately felt warmer and more intimate, and his awareness of her redoubled.

He *wanted.*

So he explained. "So am I. The problem with feasting upon *animae* is that you take on more than the energy of the life force. You absorb the attitudes and prejudices, the anger and the hatred, too."

"Not the love?"

"There isn't a lot of that on Centurios. I'm thinking that Captain Hellemut's stores were a little low, as well."

The barest smile touched Anguissa's lips then disappeared. She looked soft and seductive, yet enigmatic. He couldn't tell what she was thinking and he didn't want to slip to find out. There was something beguiling about Anguissa.

Something it might take a lifetime to understand.

"Thank you for sharing those memories," she said quietly.

"Maybe you'll have something good to tell our child about me." He lifted her hand in his, winding his fingers between hers.

"You don't have to go back to Centurios."

"I do."

"Your son."

Ryke nodded. "We had a wager, Fire-Breath, one that you won. Are you going to collect?"

Her smile was immediate, lighting her eyes with anticipation. "Is that an invitation, Soul-Stealer?"

"This is probably as close as I'll ever get to being at your mercy."

Anguissa laughed. "Oh, don't say that. I can be very persuasive." Her hand slid over his shoulder and down his chest, her gaze locked with his. "You might like it this way."

"Go ahead," he murmured, his anticipation rising. "Convince me."

Anguissa tugged off her boots. She stood then and smoothed back her snakes, then eased out of her uniform, revealing the creamy perfection of her skin. Ryke reached for his own boots but she seized his hands, guiding them to a rail over his head. "Don't make me tie you down," she purred. "You're helpless, remember?"

"I'm never helpless," he said and realized it was true.

He could always slip, and Anguissa had shown him that.

She leaned over him, soothing him with her touch. "Then pretend to be, just this once, just for me." She punctuated her request with a sweet hot kiss, one that lit a blaze deep inside him. "You might like it," she whispered.

Ryke was starting to think he just might. He knew she wouldn't try to injure him, even though she had the power to destroy him—just as he had the power to destroy her and chose not to use it. Ryke found himself capitulating to her, even though she was a dragon shifter. Her kiss became hot and hungry, proof that she had sensed the change in him, and he felt that inferno rise within him.

He recalled Mareeqa's passivity and knew that would never arouse him again.

He liked his princesses fiery now, thanks to Anguissa.

She broke their kiss and turned her back upon him, giving him a fine view as she removed his boots. She slid her hands under the top of his uniform and pushed it over his head, tossing it across the room as she surveyed him with satisfaction. Her hands were beneath the waist of his pants, her fingers awakening his skin everywhere she touched, and she worked them free as well.

He was nude before her, her smile telling him exactly what she thought of the view. She knelt on the sleeping couch beside him and it was all he could do to keep from reaching for her. She brushed her lips across his, teasing him, then closed her hand around his erection and gave him a gentle squeeze. Ryke caught his breath, Anguissa smiled, then she bent to kiss his nipple.

He gripped the bar with both hands, wanting to seize her with all his might but also needing to keep his side of the bargain. It was unnatural to just lie back and let her pleasure him, but incredibly exciting, as well. She sucked on his nipple, teasing it to a tight peak, then grazed it with her teeth. He felt himself get harder and thicker, felt the pulse in the base of his cock, and heard himself moan. Anguissa teased his nipples a little more, waiting until he moaned again before she braced herself over him and took his erection in her mouth.

Her mouth was soft and warm and sweetly teasing. He felt her tongue and thought he would explode, then opened his eyes to find a feast arrayed before his eyes. He whispered her name and Anguissa lowered herself over him. He licked her and felt her shiver and loved that he wasn't going to be passive in this encounter after all.

They teased each other for what seemed like an eternity, building the flames of desire and tormenting each other with the promise of release. Each time Ryke got close, Anguissa changed her movement, lifted her head, or paused to blow upon him. He was writhing beneath her, his muscles taut and his breath coming quickly, his pulse hammering in his ears. He was slick with her juices and hungry for more, but she denied him, making him yearn to conquer and claim.

But then she might abandon him.

He had to charm her, but charm was not a trait Ryke possessed in abundance. He was used to taking or denying, to claiming or discarding. He usually persuaded with force.

He decided to learn. He touched Anguissa more boldly, echoing her game of tease and retreat. He saw her sway over him, felt her heat rise, tasted the ardor of her arousal. He tormented her, keeping his hands on the bar, using his tongue and his lips and his teeth, even as she used the same weapons against him, until she moaned from the very bottom of her soul and shook violently.

She turned to face him, eyes flashing. "You're wicked."

"I'm trying to be persuasive," he replied and grinned at her quick intake of breath.

"I want your hands on me," she said as she moved to straddle him the other way. Ryke was quick to comply and heard himself purr as he caught her butt in his hands. "I want you to touch me, Ryke, touch me as if you can't get enough." Ryke didn't hesitate to comply. He pulled her closer, wanting her more than he'd wanted a woman before. She bent and seized his head in her hands, bracing her weight on her elbows as she kissed him.

He liked her ferocity. He liked that she demanded what she wanted.

He liked best of all that he could give it to her.

She rolled her hips and took him inside her slick heat with one smooth gesture, a move that made him catch his breath. He thought his heart might explode when she eased lower and accepted all of him. He felt himself shake, then opened his eyes to find her smiling at him.

"All mine," she whispered and he liked that just fine. He had one hand on the back of her waist and the other on the back of her neck, his embrace full of the perfection that was Anguissa. His heart thundered and he knew that no other woman would ever compare.

"For now," he countered. "Unless you come to Centurios."

"Will you make it worth my while?" she teased and Ryke inhaled sharply as she moved.

"Always, Princess," he managed to whisper, his voice hoarse, and knew it was true.

She straightened, sitting atop him proudly, her breasts inviting his caress. He cupped them, teasing their peaks, loving the view. "Convinced yet?" she asked, then stretched her arms over her head and began to ride him.

Hard. Her hips rocked and her breasts filled his hands. Her back was arched and she gasped as she rubbed herself against him. His entire body was taut, but she drove him onward, demanding more than he'd imagined he could give.

Ryke felt there wasn't enough air in the cabin. "Anguissa!" he cried but she just rode him faster, driving him on to his release. He was perilously close but he wanted them to find pleasure together. He eased one hand between them, touching her so that she moaned. She bit her lip and stretched up, her skin flushing so beautifully that Ryke didn't want to blink. Her gaze locked with his as they moved faster and faster, driving each other to the precipice.

Then he pinched her and she roared with her release, locking her legs so tightly around him that he could only do the same.

Anguissa was dizzy.

But satisfied.

Was she ever going to get enough of Ryke?

She braced her chin on her elbow and surveyed him. He was already watching her, his eyes narrowed to slits and a smile curving his firm lips. She reached out and traced the outline of his mouth with a fingertip. "Are you my HeartKeeper?"

"I don't know," he murmured, his voice rumbling in his chest and his eyes glowing. "What are the job qualifications?"

"Love, Ryke. Something you don't believe in."

He rolled then, easing her beneath himself and bracing his weight over her. "You might change my thinking about some things, Snake-Eyes, but never that." He kissed her before she could argue with him and she felt the lack of his presence in her thoughts.

"We're close to Centurios," she whispered when he lifted his head. He surveyed her, his eyes glinting, and she wondered what he was thinking.

Then he rose and tapped the comm to the deck. "How is everything, Bakiel?"

"Quiet and stable. We're within hailing distance of

the Centurios starport."

"Good." Anguissa came to Ryke's side to speak into the comm and he smiled down at her, that cocky satisfaction lighting his gaze. She watched him, anticipating his reaction to her next words. "Tell them I've come to collect the bounty on Ryke. I think the live one, but I could still change my mind if he doesn't behave."

"If you're going to be an opportunist, Snake-Eyes," Ryke said, with a thread of humor in his tone, "you should collect the higher bounty, the one for delivering me dead."

Anguissa smiled because she saw his confidence that she wouldn't do that. "But that won't answer the question, Ryke. When someone wants me dead, I like to know why. Don't you?" She gave him a look, watching relief settle through him, then stretched to kiss his cheek. "I'm going to put you in shackles," she whispered.

"Not a chance," he replied, sealing his words with a kiss. "I've had my share of being controlled."

"But..."

"But nothing," he said, interrupting her. "I might need to defend us."

Anguissa had her doubts about that plan and didn't hide them. "It would be good if you could keep from looking like a conquering hero."

Ryke chuckled. "There's only so much of my nature I can change, Princess."

Then she left the cabin, striding toward the deck.

She felt him watching her go.

But she didn't hear him in her thoughts. They'd already parted ways, for all intents and purposes, and that saddened Anguissa more than she knew it should.

She didn't love Ryke.

She couldn't love Ryke.

She wouldn't.

Chapter Eight

enturios.

A planet wreathed in fog and shadows. It appeared to be veiled in smoke. Even the starport looked menacing. It was dark and heavily armed, its design both antique and heavy. It could have been brute force in orbit.

A planet with *umbros* in charge. Anguissa shivered. She'd checked the reference on her personal device and hadn't found it reassuring either.

Centurios: A planet in the Vergon system in the Qaton sector. Although many sentient species make their home on this, the only habitable planet in its system, the reputation of one species is known throughout the galaxy. Umbros, a class of predators with a taste for either blood or souls, originate on Centurios. Despite being a minority of the population, umbros have been the planet's overlords for more than half of the planet's history, maintaining authority with a combination of terror and violence. The umbros subsist upon the blood or soul, whether the host is living or recently deceased. It is believed that their appetites were established when the various peoples of Centurios waged frequent war and some of them consumed corpses because of widespread famine.

There are more than eleven other castes in this highly organized and divided society, including the pale custos who each serve the will of a single umbro, even to their own detriment. The planet itself is over half water, dominated by a single large and predominantly flat land mass, with the capital city at its center. Centurios maintains a starport but given the widespread fear of their overlords—and the tendency of umbros to infiltrate alien societies and feed, thus leaving a trail of victims—the ability of Centurios to conduct trade has been severely curtailed. The relative net worth of Centurios has declined as a result, as had the standard of living of its populace.

Ryke was sitting on the transport deck with his hands behind his back. They weren't bound as he wouldn't agree to that, but someone might be fooled at a glance. His head was slightly bowed and he did look a little bit less confident than usual.

Anguissa still wasn't sure that anyone would be convinced he was a prisoner, but she didn't want their last discussion to be an argument.

Either way, he'd be home soon, and she'd be heading back to Incendium.

Maybe on the way, she'd figure out what to do with the payload of the Archangel.

And what to do about Bond.

First things first.

"Any reply to our hail?" she asked Bakiel.

The *custo* shook his head. "Silence."

Ryke frowned and Anguissa knew he was going to try to take command. She got abruptly to her feet, seized a length of cloth, and marched toward him. He smiled at her, his gaze assessing, but his smile faded when she snapped the cloth around his head and blindfolded him. He paled and she knew he was shaken.

Still, he stayed out of her mind.

Was something wrong? Anguissa dismissed the idea as soon as she had it. Ryke wouldn't lie to her. It was a gift to make their inevitable parting easier.

"Finally, you look like a captive," she teased quietly

instead.

"Snake-Eyes..." he growled.

"A feint is only as good as the performance, Ryke." Anguissa whispered to him, knowing he was struggling against some dark experience but confident that he could persevere. "You've survived worse. Trust me on this, or we're all dead."

He exhaled, shaking a little, then lifted his head proudly. His posture was the perfect blend of resignation and bravado. His trust humbled her and fortified her determination to succeed.

"But they can't be gone," she said, raising her voice and aware that their conversation might be monitored. "We have indications of life forms on the station..."

She was interrupted by an authoritative voice that boomed from the comm and proved that her assumption was correct. "Magnetawan, this is Centurios Starport. Identify the three life forms aboard."

No greeting. No polite salute or diplomacy. Anguissa bristled.

"Greetings," she replied, her tone cool. She didn't look at either Bakiel or Ryke. "I am Captain Anguissa of the Gloria Furore, coming to collect the bounty offered for Ryke of Centurios. His *custo* is aboard, as well."

There was a moment of silence, which Anguissa chose to interpret as surprise. "Ryke of Centurios is said to be dead."

"He's not. He's my captive." There was no reply, so Anguissa pushed a little. "Do you deny that there is a posted bounty?"

"Show him."

The abrupt replies annoyed Anguissa, but she hid her reaction as well as she could. Her mother, Ignita, always said that there was no cause for rudeness and in this moment, Anguissa could only agree.

She gestured to Ryke. "He's on the transport deck,

ready to be delivered as soon as the payment is made." The input tracked her gesture and displayed Ryke to whoever was on the other side of the comm. "I assume you want a voice imprint for verification."

"Yes. We do not transfer funds without verification, Captain Anguissa."

Ryke yelped, as if he'd been given an electric prod, which Anguissa thought was truly inspired. Then he continued in a low growl. "Anyone I know in command today?"

The display flickered to life and Anguissa was shocked by the pallor of the face that filled it. She wasn't nearly as surprised as Bakiel, though, who caught his breath and turned even more white than usual. Ryke stiffened, apparently aware of Bakiel's reaction even though he couldn't see it.

The man on the display looked slightly familiar, but Anguissa didn't manage to place him before Bakiel whispered "Titus!"

"Titus?" Ryke echoed. "How did you end up with this responsibility? It's a little beneath the tasks of the emperor's *custo*. Have the ranks of my father's soldiers diminished this much?"

The fair man smirked. "Much has changed in your absence."

"I'm surprised that my father offered a reward for my return," Ryke continued, looking about as vulnerable and defeated as a champion of the universe. Anguissa was glad that he was blindfolded and noted that Titus didn't seem surprised by his manner. "I never expected to be ransomed, given that I was an outlaw on Centurios."

"You were missed, Ryke," another man said, and Titus was replaced on the display by an older man. He shared Ryke's proud profile and noble bearing, and Anguissa recognized him from Ryke's memory. Even though he was older, he appeared to be virile, and his eyes shone with the same glimmer that illuminated Ryke's. His voice was low and melodious and Anguissa might have been charmed.

If she hadn't noticed the harsh line of his mouth or the hardness in his gaze.

If she didn't know better.

Ryke's father smiled a little, a cool expression that didn't soften his features at all. "Is that so hard to believe, my son?"

"Father!"

"None other." The older man turned, apparently looking at his *custo*, and spoke with authority. "Begin the teleport, Titus. Bring my son home."

The deck began to shimmer and Bakiel stepped toward Ryke.

"I think you're forgetting something," Anguissa said, keeping one hand on the controls of the teleport on the Magnetawan. "I haven't been paid the bounty I'm owed."

Ryke's father met her gaze steadily. "That payment won't be necessary, Captain Anguissa. The Gloria Furore has posted a bounty upon you." His smile grew colder. "We don't bargain with criminals."

"I don't have to surrender Ryke, then."

His eyes narrowed. "I'm prepared to allow you an increment of amnesty in exchange for Ryke's return. Run while you can, Captain Anguissa."

"I want the bounty paid," Anguissa insisted.

She would have argued further but a dark chill seized her mind. She gasped and staggered at its abrupt intrusion. It was rough and forceful, lingering only long enough to compel her to release the teleport.

I will have my son.

Anguissa staggered under the influence of the anger and hatred of Ryke's father's mind.

"Bakiel!" Ryke shouted and Anguissa realized the teleport had begun.

"Ryke!" she cried, before the pain in her mind was so great that tears slipped from the corners of her eyes. She fell to the deck, fighting the agony.

I could kill you, abomination, but I choose to let you survive. Run while you can and be grateful for my mercy.

Anger filled Anguissa, along with a resolve to destroy the invader at any price.

Then abruptly, the invading force was gone.

Ryke was gone, too, no more than a shimmer left of him on the teleport deck.

And the echo of his last call.

The *custo* lunged for the teleport, so stricken to be left behind that Anguissa activated the teleport of her own will. She felt violated, after having experienced Ryke's father, and was struck by the contrast between father and son. Ryke would never have been so abusive. She had no doubt that Centurios would be a treacherous place for her, and wanted only to leave.

"Go with him, Bakiel," she murmured.

"Come with me."

"Never!"

The *custo* turned to her and swallowed, then bowed his head. "But you are Ryke's *luxa*. We need you!"

Anguissa wasn't immune to his entreaty but she knew that the only result of her following Ryke would be her own death. Her departure would ensure that the prophecy didn't come true, but she knew that Ryke didn't believe in the prophecy or her role. He didn't believe in love. He wanted only to be with his son and back on Centurios. He had what he desired and maybe she would forget him in time.

Even if she was afraid she was abandoning her HeartKeeper, she had to defend the child she carried. That would have to be her legacy from Ryke.

"Farewell, Bakiel. I hope you always believe in a better future." Anguissa touched the control and Bakiel sparkled as the teleport began.

"Farewell, Captain Anguissa," Bakiel whispered. She watched until every last glimmer had extinguished, even after the console showed that the teleport was complete. Then she sighed and set her course for Incendium.

Home.

A host of other problems and a lot of solitude. The Magnetawan felt empty, as empty as her mind without Ryke, but Anguissa knew she had to get used to that. She fought an uncharacteristic urge to shed a tear or two, ignoring the view of the starport as she charted her course.

And that was her mistake. She didn't see the attack launch, until the Magnetawan's defense systems were deployed and sirens began to blare.

Ryke's reaction to reaching his destination was mixed. He was glad he'd succeeded in returning alive. He was relieved to be back on Centurios, but the familiar elements of his home planet were less reassuring than he might have hoped.

He felt uneasy, leaving Anguissa, and the farther he was from her side, the harder it was to believe that she had twisted his thinking that much.

What if she *was* his *luxa?*

What if he wasn't just abandoning his child but throwing away the future, for Centurios as well as himself? Bakiel's final words resonated in Ryke's mind with inescapable power.

He was going to miss the daring dragon shifter princess and starship captain.

Even if she didn't follow anyone's rules.

Maybe because of that.

As soon as Bakiel arrived, the pair of them were herded toward a shuttle to the capital city, where his father awaited him. Ryke's father and Titus weren't on the station, of course, but safe in the imperial palace. Ryke was keenly aware of how worn the equipment was around him, how ancient the technology, how gaunt and wary the people of Centurios had become. Although Centurios hadn't been overwhelmingly prosperous in recent memory, it had become significantly more impoverished in his absence.

He was glad that Anguissa had sent Bakiel after him and looking forward to seeing his son again. He forced himself to concentrate on the positive.

He refused to think about Anguissa sailing into the void and disappearing from his life forever.

"His *luxa?*" the guard ushering them to the shuttle whispered to Bakiel.

Ryke glanced up. Bakiel's last words on the Magnetawan had been transmitted to the starport but had been uttered so quietly that he was sure no one had heard them.

It appeared that he was wrong.

Bakiel only nodded, but Ryke watched the awe dawn in the guard's eyes. It was followed by speculation and hope, a combination that worried Ryke.

"It was an illusion," he said crisply, wanting to stop rumor before it started. He'd be even more of a failure if they thought he'd betrayed them, even if it was just a story.

The guard looked between the two of them, then turned his attention to his task when Bakiel's expression didn't change. Ryke gave his *custo* a look but Bakiel was unrepentant. *'Luxa,"* he mouthed, his eyes shining. *'Don't let her go."*

Ryke halted. He wasn't an impulsive man. He wasn't a dreamer and he didn't believe in fairy tales. But he wanted to be with Anguissa more than anything he'd wanted before.

He decided to trust his heart.

"Wait!" he called and pivoted to look at the display. He expected to see that the Magnetawan sailing toward a wormhole that would take it closer to Incendium, having been given right of way.

Instead, he saw the freighter being attacked.

"No!" he roared, lunging back toward the deck. "The Magnetawan should have safe passage. Captain Anguissa brought me home!"

"The emperor commanded the attack," the captain of the shuttle informed him and Ryke watched in horror as the Magnetawan was subjected to a barrage of fire. "It's only rational to eliminate a criminal wanted by the Gloria Furore."

"No!" Ryke cried again and tried to push the weapons master from his console. They fought, scuffling on the floor as Ryke tried to gain control despite his opponent's strength. Some of the men continued their jobs, ignoring the fight, while the men closest to Ryke watched in shock and horror.

"He's lost his mind," whispered the commander.

"He's found his heart," Bakiel said with confidence. "And his *luxa*. Ryke is the one foretold who will bring change to Centurios."

A ripple of excitement passed through the crew on deck, but Ryke didn't care. He punched his opponent in the nose and flung him to one side. He could have slipped. He could have manipulated the man or destroyed him, but Ryke refused to do as much. He seized control of the console when the weapons master held up his hands in defeat, but so many rounds had already been fired. He managed to stop the onslaught, but feared it was too late.

The hull of the Magnetawan exploded and a large chunk of the fuselage fell away. Anguissa appeared to be firing back. She gave as good as she got, but the Magnetawan wasn't as heavily armed as the Centurios starport.

Nor was its armor sufficient to defend it against such a concerted attack at close proximity. His fists clenched as the freighter fell, tumbling to a lower orbit.

Had Anguissa done that?

Was it a feint?

Was she choosing to die rather than be captured? There was no chance of the Magnetawan escaping that attack in a condition that would allow it to jump. And she knew about the opinion of her kind on Centurios. He watched the wreckage fall and felt as if a precious gem had been torn away from him.

He liked to think that he could have made his peace with never seeing her again, that just knowing she was alive, taking bold chances somewhere in the universe, would have been enough for him.

He couldn't bear that she would die.

He hated that there was nothing he could do to save her.

He couldn't have blamed her for not wanting to carry the child of an *umbro*, not when she'd been so betrayed. His father had broken his word to allow her safe passage. Ryke's heart tightened as he watched the freighter disintegrate into wreckage and fall toward the surface. The metal began to heat to red-hot with the friction of re-entry, and he wondered if any part of it would survive.

Certainly, his *luxa* wouldn't.

"Anguissa," he whispered, becoming aware of the stares of those around him.

Then a fury seized his mind, like a cold hand sheathed in steel. He screamed as his brain clenched and an icy whisper slipped into his thoughts.

You will deny her. His father commanded. *You will call her an abomination.*

Ryke recoiled in horror and disgust. His father had slipped into him!

It was taboo. It was wrong.

It was a violation of everything they were.

No umbro *should slip into another* umbro. He managed to protest.

His father laughed. *I do what I want. I take what is mine. You will do what you are told to do.*

Ryke braced himself and reached abruptly into his father's mind, using surprise to seek evidence that Anguissa had been right. He found it in abundance, the scheme to discredit him, the invitation that brought the Gloria Furore in to raid, the insistence that Ryke not be ransomed, the command that he be tortured and broken.

His own son.

Because Ryke was the prophesied *umbro* who could change everything and his father knew it.

First, Anguissa would die, then Ryke, then probably his son.

His father fought back with sudden strength, flinging Ryke from his thoughts and following his retreat like a missile. His will blossomed in Ryke's thoughts and Ryke feinted, with all the speed and grace of a dragon princess. He pretended to be overwhelmed and even fell to the deck of the starport, twisting like a man possessed.

Denounce her.

My son? Ryke kept his tone weak and humble, as if this was his dying breath. He could feel the blood seeping from one of his ears and knew his father would kill him as soon as he did as ordered.

Safely at his studies in Greater Andal. Do as I ask and I will tell him that you returned a hero, but too damaged by torture to survive. Do what I ask and your memory will be honored.

Ryke whimpered as if capitulating. He felt his father's amusement, his pride in his power, and braced himself for the worst.

Never! Ryke bellowed then he flung himself back at his father's mind. He seized at the root of it and squeezed, twisting and tearing, a will for destruction filling him.

His father was taken by surprise and by the time he tried to fight back, it was too late. Ryke could feel the blood seeping from his father's body. He heard the cell walls and vessels bursting from the pressure and he heard the moan from the depths of his father's being.

He knew what his father expected, but Ryke refused to feast on his father's *anima*. There were some forces that should be lost forever and his father's hatred was one of them.

He waited until there was no chance of recovery, then abandoned his father, straightening on the deck of the starport, knowing his gaze was resolute.

"My father has been taken ill," he said with calm authority. "I am taking command of the starport."

"All hail the new emperor," Bakiel said with reverence and bowed deeply. "The time of the prophecy has come." The entire crew bowed deeply.

"Can the Magnetawan be saved?" he asked. "Anguissa is my *luxa*. Spare no effort to bring the light safely into the darkness."

"It is too close to the surface, sir. Her fate is sealed."

The Magnetawan was still spiraling downward, only a fraction of its former self. A plume of fire trailed behind it, which Ryke could see on the display and he wished that it was dragon fire instead of the vessel's destruction. He reached for Anguissa, hoping she wasn't already dead, and slipped.

He had to tell her that he'd realized the truth, even if it was the last thing he said to her.

Knock, knock, Snake-Eyes.

Anguissa was strapped down and curled tightly into a ball, eyes closed against the heat that consumed what remained of the Magnetawan. There was nothing to be gained by shifting shape, which was a novel experience for her. To be smaller was better as the freighter fell into pieces.

She'd made a mistake, not wanting to reveal the truth of her nature too soon, and the Magnetawan had betrayed her. Shields had automatically deployed as the ship was damaged and she was sealed into an area a fraction of the deck's size. It was too small for her to shift and too armored for her to break free of it. She was sure it would be her coffin and that she would run out of oxygen sealed inside it.

Then Ryke whispered in her thoughts.

She'd never been so glad to hear the voice of another in her life.

Soul-snatcher!

She heard his chuckle and wanted to curl up in the sound forever. *You were right, Anguissa. My father betrayed me and now I've paid him back.*

He's dead?

Nearly. I've let nature take its course.

Will you be emperor?

Maybe. What's important is that I wanted you to know that Bakiel was right, too.

How so?

Luxa. The word was murmured softly, his voice so deep and filled with affection that Anguissa nearly wept.

HeartKeeper.

I wanted you to know that I love you.

I love you, too, Ryke.

Feel like taking a chance?

More of one than loving an umbro?

Ryke didn't answer that, but continued quickly. *There are two fighters en route toward you. Is there any chance you could survive if they blew what's left of the Magnetawan apart? You're still above atmosphere but...*

I can spin an orb. Anguissa interrupted him. *Do it.*

You're sure? It sounded like an acquired skill.

I'm good, Ryke. Trust me.

I do.

And anything has to be better than dying in this piece of junk you call a starship.

It's risky, Princess.

Everything worth doing is.

Anguissa heard Ryke giving commands and knew she'd convinced him. She closed her eyes, praying as she never had before. She realized it was because she had something to live for, something more important than her own survival or even that of the Archangel.

"Impact minus five."

Anguissa listened to Ryke, knowing that if his voice was the last thing she heard, that would be just fine.

"Four. Three. Two. One."

The Magnetawan exploded in fire, cracking open like an egg. Anguissa could see and feel the flames that consumed it, but she shifted shape as soon as there was space. She surged upward, through the fire and flame, beating her wings as she rolled into a perfect orb. The orb shone in the light of the rising sun, turned gold by the dawn, and Anguissa flew toward the land mass she could see in the distance, her heart beating with joy.

You're beautiful, Princess. I can see you, gleaming like obsidian.

The sun is rising, Ryke.

Yes, it is! Welcome to a new era for Centurios, Anguissa. He paused and his next words were husky. *Wait for me.*

Always.

Anguissa flew to the starport, knowing that she was being watched. She descended slowly, choosing her location, knowing it would be a few hours before Ryke's shuttle reached the surface. When she saw a boy shielding his eyes to look up at her, she guessed who he might be.

He was taller than he'd been in Ryke's memory and

more gangly, a boy on the cusp of becoming a man. He stood like Ryke, though, tall and straight, and waited without fear when she descended toward him.

Anyone you know? She thought the question to Ryke, liking the huskiness of his voice when he replied.

You know it is. Of course.

Of course?

Of all the people in Centurios, only you would find my son first.

It's a question of focus, Ryke.

It's a question of destiny.

I thought you didn't believe in that.

You've changed my mind about a lot of things, Snake Eyes.

I've only just started.

Ryke laughed. *I know. You're my* luxa, *Anguissa, the one who will bring the light and the healing.*

Anguissa smiled that he'd called her by her name three times in succession, as well as acknowledged the force between them. *Luxa.* HeartKeeper. Two interpretations of the same concept from two very different societies.

Anguissa heard Ryke's announcement of her role in his life as she descended steadily toward his son. She heard his command that she should not be injured and she saw the wonder on the faces of those who gathered around his son. They fell to their knees when she landed, but the boy's gaze was unswerving. His eyes widened as Anguissa shifted to her human form and she smiled at him.

"You're Ryke's son."

"And you're the *luxa* foretold," he replied, his gaze brightening with anticipation. "Will you take me for a dragon ride?"

Anguissa laughed aloud, because her reception at Centurios was exactly the opposite of what she'd dreaded.

Going to stay, Princess?

Only if you pledge to be my HeartKeeper, Ryke. Our child deserves no less.

His reply was a lazy growl of satisfaction. *I believe that can be arranged.*

• • •

CELI'S QUEST

The Dragons of Incendium 8

DEBORAH COOKE

PROLOGUE

Celo didn't have to go to the capital city of Regalia to know that his brother Venero had triumphed in the Queen's Grotto. He felt a shudder of relief pass through the land and knew his brother Urbanus was dead. He saw the dark fog rise from the valleys and felt the air clear, and knew his mother, Arcana, was dead. He awoke to find spring flowers blooming, the forest floor covered with yellow and white blooms, and knew Venero had taken the throne.

The old stories of the kingdom resonating with the truth of the king's character were all true. Celo heard the creatures of the forest whisper to each other of new light and knew that the dragon princess Gemma was Venero's queen.

It could have been the first spring ever. The sunlight was brighter. The new growth was greener. The birds' songs were more beautiful and lasted longer. The forest abounded with new life and the skies were gloriously blue. Celo himself felt his heart lighten. He began to whistle again and to dream. His refuge had its pleasures but also its limitations.

The fact was that the short time he'd spent in Gemma's company had made the deficit of his life painfully clear.

He missed the company of women. He missed how

they laughed. He missed how pretty they were. He missed how he felt when a woman smiled at him or laughed at one of his comments. He missed that tingle of awareness and the sense of possibility. He began to notice the birds and animals in their courtship rituals and to feel the solitude of his refuge more keenly.

Gemma wasn't for him, he knew that, but she wasn't the only woman in the universe. He shaved the long growth from his chin and spared some coin for new clothes, then ventured into the local village.

To his surprise, he was welcomed.

To his further surprise, he found himself returning at intervals and looking forward to it. He told himself that it was because he no longer feared repercussions from his family, but it was more than that and he knew it.

It was in town that Celo heard the details about the glorious wedding and sumptuous coronation. As convinced as he had been that he'd never return to Regalia's capital city again, Celo began to consider it. He knew that Venero and Gemma would welcome him, but something kept him from setting out for the castle.

Celo realized why one bright summer morning. He left his hut to fetch water from the stream, whistling as had become his habit.

"It is time," said the raven he called Nix, sparing him a knowing look.

"You must go south," said the hare, then sprang into the forest.

An owl descended and landed on his shoulder. Celo looked up at the bird, for it should have been asleep at this hour.

The owl winked. "You were born for this quest."

Celo felt a strange sense that he'd been waiting for this very message. A quest? But to where? And why?

A flock of white birds took flight ahead of him, swirling together as if to draw his gaze. When they abruptly scattered, he found himself looking at the distant peak of Mount Draco, the highest peak on Regalia, its summit glittering with ice.

Celo's heart stopped then raced again. He'd always been fascinated by the mountain and had been glad that the location of his refuge allowed him glimpses of its majesty. It had never been scaled. Indeed, few had ever ventured near it. It was too cold. Too high. Too distant. It was far beyond even the Queen's Grotto, remote and unyielding.

And there were stories, tales of the winds around it being filled with the voices of ghosts, stories of men driven mad after just one night in its shadow, legends of fierce beasts that lived deep beneath the mountain's roots.

Yet when the owl spoke to him, Celo recognized the truth. Mount Draco was his destiny, and now that the shadow had lifted from Regalia, it was time for him to embark upon the quest that might be his last.

He didn't know what he would discover, either on the mountain or about himself. That was part of the adventure.

He stayed at the river only long enough to wash and drink, then he returned to his hut to pack his few belongings. It was early in the morning on a fine clear day.

Nix was right. It was time to go.

CHAPTER ONE

Celo's beard had grown again and the soles of his boots had holes by the time he reached the foot of Mount Draco. He had walked through the spring and the summer, too. The air was cold at nights now, and he knew there soon would be snow. The animals had grown their winter coats, the hares now white, and many had built nests for the winter. He was leaner and stronger than he had been, and though he was tired, he felt robust. He was excited to come close to his goal.

His curiosity was alight. He imagined countless possibilities of what he might find, and his dreams were filled with promise.

Celo climbed up Mount Draco's flanks as the sun was setting and found shelter in the last copse of pine trees. He was surprised that he heard no ghostly whispers in his pine bower. Perhaps the stories about the mountain were untrue.

Or maybe they weren't true any longer.

Maybe even more had changed in Regalia with Arcana's death. He wondered if there was a catalog anywhere of his mother's spells and feared that only Urbanus had known them all. They were stored in the Queen's Grotto, but coded. Would anyone ever unravel them all? He had thought long and hard about the

Queen's Grotto during his walk, weighing the possible repercussions of simply destroying it and breaking all of the spells at once.

Was it possible that there were any good spells there?

There was ice on the river in the morning, and Celo broke through it to refresh himself. Snow covered the rocks around him and dusted the branches of the trees. He stood and ate the last of his provisions, surveying the mountain that rose high before him. There was no path, of course, given that no one climbed it, but he could see a natural course in the rock, one that snaked toward the summit. It was barren on each side and he knew he would feel every breath of wind. Celo stood amidst the last trees and took a deep breath of their scent, then packed away one last piece of dry bread and began to walk.

Although he couldn't see any birds or other creatures, he had the sense that he wasn't alone. He could almost, but not quite, feel the presence of another creature near him. That he couldn't clearly discern its thoughts made him wonder about it.

Were the stories of ancient beasts beneath the mountain true?

Perhaps if it was an old, old species, or an alien one, its thoughts would make no sense to Celo. He was skeptical of that possibility, though, as he clearly understood all the creatures of the forest.

Could it shield its mind? That was generally a mark of sophistication or some magical ability. Were the stories of ancient beasts beneath the mountain told to disguise the presence of a sorcerer?

That was a more compelling possibility. Perhaps his mother's death had broken a spell that had trapped another sorcerer. She'd never been interested in competition. Gemma and Venero might have broken the spell inadvertently, or not realized what it was.

Celo tried to remember every story he'd ever heard about sorcerers on Regalia but couldn't think of one that didn't feature his brother Urbanus.

He scrambled his way higher and higher as the sun rose. He scraped his hands, he stubbed his toe, and he broke into a sweat from exertion. The mountain stretched higher, and he could see that its summit wasn't one peak but a line of jagged outcroppings. He reached a precipice and leaned against the mountain to catch his breath, turning to look back over the wilderness of Regalia.

It was beautiful. So filled with bounty and wildlife. Celo knew the kingdom would prosper beneath Venero's hand. It was filled with opportunity and possibility, ripe for a guiding hand like that of his brother. Celo eyed the clouds that were gathering and wondered if he would find some shelter on the mountainside for the night.

Suddenly, the icy ledge beneath his feet shifted.

His heart leaped in terror that he would fall.

He scrambled to regain his footing as an avalanche of ice rained upon his head. It spilled over him, cracking on his shoulders. The mountainside was a sheer drop, and the fall would be long enough to kill him. He grabbed and snatched, his feet slipping and his heart pounding, until he finally caught hold of a shard of stone. He spun and grabbed another rock that held fast, and was splayed against the mountain, hanging by his hands.

Celo held on tightly as the stone fell down the mountainside. He watched the ice that had been under his feet shatter into pieces on the rocks below. He exhaled in relief, found a ledge for one foot, then felt a pulse beneath the stone.

The hair stood up on his nape.

Behind him, the mountain rippled.

Celo glanced over his shoulder, certain he had imagined the heartbeat so loud that it made the very mountain vibrate, then stared.

The mountain had changed. It was still pale grey, but he could see the outline of large scales on its surface. Each was as big as a warrior, each one tipped in silver. He climbed onto a ledge so that he had a free hand, then ran that hand over the closest scale. It wasn't rock. He would have stepped back but he was on a narrow ledge. When the mountain shifted once more, shuddering to its roots as if shaken by an earthquake, Celo cried out as he lost his footing again.

When he managed to find another small ledge for his feet, he closed his eyes for a minute to catch his breath. He heard the ice fall away in a torrent, scattering and shattering. He opened his eyes to find that all of the snow had been cast off to reveal the mountain beneath.

Celo blinked, unable to believe his eyes. Below him, the mountain was the shape of a massive silver dragon, covered in those scales. He could see its feet and its belly. It was crouched, its tail curled around its body. He looked up and saw its back rising high above him, and managed to glimpse its head resting on its forearms.

Celo realized he was standing on the knee of the beast, and that he had only climbed a small fraction of its height. The line of outcroppings that he thought led to its summit looked like scales along its spine. The path he'd followed had been the curve of its folded leg. He had slept in that pine forest nestled between its tail and its back claw.

His first thought was that the dragon was a natural formation, but that was impossible. There was too much detail.

His second was that some great artist had carved it from the rock, accentuating the features created by nature. Perhaps a team of craftsmen had done it, for the task would have been massive.

But why had he never heard of it before?

A rumble emitted from deep within mountain, reminding Celo of bears awakening in the spring. He saw a waft of steam emanate from part of the mountain far ahead and noted the resemblance of that area to a snout, pierced by a pair of nostrils.

He froze at the realization that the smoke had come from those very holes.

Then just above it, the rock cracked and an eye opened, an orange eye that might have been made of fire.

That fiery gaze locked upon him.

When the mountain dragon smiled and its eyes gleamed, Celo leaped from the great knee and ran for his life.

Celo didn't get far. He jumped from the dragon's knee but before he landed, one great claw snatched him out of the air. His heart raced in terror even as he struggled for freedom. Even falling from this height had to be better than whatever fate a dragon had planned for him.

He was lifted high as he fought against the grasp of that great claw. He was held tightly but not squeezed. He couldn't escape, but he wasn't hurt. That reassured him a little, until he was held up to that massive blazing eye.

The orb was bigger than he was tall, the pupil a vertical slit that was blacker than midnight. The iris was in motion in a mesmerizing way, a hundred shades of orange, yellow, and red, moving like the flames of an inferno. He had the curious thought that he could have stepped through that dark pupil, as if it were a doorway into the dragon's mind.

The dragon smiled. "A perilous adventure indeed," it mused, a waft of smoke rising from its nostrils.

"He," the dragon rumbled. Celo realized it—he—had discerned his thoughts and hastily tried to shield his mind.

"There is no point," the dragon said calmly. "I have

the patience and the persistence to solve any riddle."

"Of course." Celo tried to bow and managed only to incline his head. Deference seemed like a wise plan, given the size of the dragon—and the fact that Celo couldn't read his thoughts at all. "I apologize for disturbing your sleep. I didn't realize the mountain was alive."

The dragon appeared to be amused. "All mountains are alive, but some of them have forgotten how to awaken."

"Would you be Draco, then?"

That smile broadened lazily and the eyes gleamed. "I would. And you?"

"Celo. Prince Celo of Regalia."

The dragon studied him again. "You're not who I expected. Are you lost?"

Who had Draco expected?

"No, I don't think so. The raven told me it was time and the birds showed me my destination."

"Well, then, things must have changed." The dragon seemed to be considering this. His expression and relaxed manner indicated that the process could take a while. Celo was interested in learning Draco's plans for him a little sooner than that.

"May I ask a question?"

"You just did."

"Another?"

Draco chuckled. "Again, you just did."

Celo cleared his throat and avoided the trap for the third time. "Who were you expecting?"

"The spellbreaker, of course. Such heroes are inclined to collect their rewards." Draco's eyes sparkled.

Celo wondered what the reward might be. "Would you have given it?"

"Of course!"

"How do you know I didn't do it?"

"There's no smell of spellcraft about you, nor do I

detect that you've visited that horrific cavern."

Celo shuddered at even the oblique reference to the Queen's Grotto. "I haven't."

"Yet the spellbreaker did, because the spell was there."

"How do you know that?"

Draco's expression was pitying. "Aren't all spells still kept there?"

He knew something of Regalia, then. "It must have been my brother, Venero. He was going there with Gemma."

"Gemma?" Draco's eyes lit with the sparks of a brighter flame.

Celo saw no reason to hold back any detail he knew, especially as Draco could just read his mind. "One of the dragon princesses of Incendium. She said Venero was the Carrier of the Seed. He seemed to be taken with her, as well, particularly as she had started to break the spell cast upon him by his twin brother, Urbanus."

Draco nodded. "I approve of dragon princesses who break spells. What happened?"

"I think Urbanus and our mother Arcana are dead."

"And Venero?"

"He is king now, and Gemma his queen."

Draco lifted a brow. "Will he be a good king?"

"Yes." Celo had no hesitation.

"Who is Gemma's father?"

"King Ouros of Incendium."

"And his father?"

Celo wasn't certain whether Draco had slept through Ouros' administration or whether this was a test. It felt like a test, so he tried to recall the history of the royal family of Incendium. "Torris, I believe."

"His father?"

"Dracon."

"A fine name." Draco chuckled. "His father?"

"Ardeo was the fourth dragon King of Incendium. He had a twin brother, Incantos."

"Ardeo and Incantos," Draco repeated, his tone thoughtful.

Did he remember them or not?

"How long have you been sleeping here?" Celo asked, feeling a little bolder since he hadn't been injured yet. "Ardeo and Incantos were born almost eleven hundred Incendium years ago."

"Longer than that, clearly," Draco said with a tinge of impatience. "Their father?"

Unfortunately, Celo didn't recall all of the early kings, so he jumped back to the first one. "Did you know Scintillon, the first dragon King of Incendium? He claimed the throne in what became Incendium year one, almost two thousand years ago."

"Scintillon, yes." Draco nodded. "I remember him as a young slave with a human wife." He mused before he continued. "Primula. That was her name. His owner used to beat her to ensure Scintillon's obedience. I never thought he'd amount to much."

"He founded a dynasty." Celo took a breath. "He exiled those who protested against him here, to Regalia."

"When things became more noisy." Draco arched a brow. "And a young rogue who called himself the King of Regalia took umbrage at my request for quiet and solitude."

"That's when you went to sleep?"

"I was enchanted then, yes." Draco leaned closer to sniff Celo, and Celo tried to keep from recoiling. "Being a prince of Regalia must make you a descendant of that...individual."

"But not a Spellcaster." Celo wriggled free and held up his hands. "I refused to learn the family craft."

Draco's eyes glittered and his voice dropped low. "The ability to cast magic is inherent and often inherited.

I smell it in your blood."

Celo was much less certain of his own safety, given Draco's expression. "I can read the thoughts of others. That's the extent of my gift."

Draco's gaze hardened. "Prove it. Read mine."

It was a test and a good one. Celo had been trying to read Draco's mind ever since the dragon's eye had opened with no results at all. He'd thought it a good idea to try to determine what the dragon intended to do to him, not that he would have been able to do much about it.

He hadn't been able to discern one thing.

He tried again, but might have been attempting to scale the face of a sheer rock wall. He strained, he stretched, he tried to sneak, but he was confounded by every technique he'd found effective in the past.

Draco's eyes shone, and Celo knew he wasn't surprised.

"I can't," he admitted.

"No. But the raven talks to you?"

"Not often, but he does. He told me it was time."

"Well, that must mean something. The most reliable sources of news for me have always been the ravens." Draco nodded slowly, his gaze sliding over the view. His voice rumbled when he was pensive and sent vibrations through Celo. "He must have sent you for a reason."

Celo hoped that was a good thing. "Then you aren't going to eat me?"

"You'd be barely a bite."

"Burn me or destroy me?"

Draco's smile widened, revealing an astonishing array of sharp white teeth. His breath was hot and his eyes shone. "No, I want something far more important from you."

Celo's hands clenched in fear. "What's that?"

"I want to give you the spellbreaker's reward."

Celo felt sudden trepidation. What was the spellbreaker owed? It might not be a good reward. It might be harmful to his health. It might shake his mind or rattle his bones or leave him scarred or...

"What's that?" Celo asked, hearing that his own voice was no more than a squeak.

"I want you to listen to a story, of course."

Celo barely believed his own ears.

But Draco moved and the wind ruffled through Celo's hair. The dragon settled himself again and put Celo down. His forelegs rested along the rocky ground, defining a hollow that blocked the wind. Celo shivered a little and Draco noticed. He reared back and lifted the claw that had held Celo, reaching down to seize a dead tree from the flat land that surrounded his resting place.

He broke it into pieces with one claw, the logs and sticks falling into a pile in the clearing before himself. He pushed a pile together, then breathed a plume of fire upon it. The dry wood crackled as it lit, a bonfire casting golden light and welcome heat around it. Draco settled again, forming that hollow with his legs again and Celo sat on one talon, holding his hands to the blaze.

"Thank you very much," he said, and Draco inclined his head slightly.

Celo was still hungry but he was warm, and that was enough of an improvement that he could listen to a story.

"I believe you still have a piece of bread," the dragon reminded him.

"I wouldn't want to be rude," Celo said but the dragon smiled.

"I don't want hunger to affect your attention. Go ahead."

Celo pulled out the last piece of bread from his purse and ate it slowly.

"In the beginning, there was the fire," Draco said, his

voice a low rumble that Celo could feel as well as hear.

Draco's back loomed high over Celo, and one wing was slightly unfolded to provide shelter. Instead of seeing the stars overhead, Celo watched the light from the fire play over the silver membrane of the underside of Draco's wing. The dragon looked out over Regalia—which Celo couldn't see because of the height of Draco's foreleg—his eyes narrowed to bright slits.

"And the fire burned hot because it was cradled by the earth. The fire burned bright because it was nurtured by the air. The fire burned lower only when it was quenched by the water. And these were the four elements of divine design, of which all would be built and with which all would be destroyed. And the elements were the cornerstones of the material universe and it was good."

Celo felt himself almost lulled to sleep by the dragon's deep voice and the heat of the fire. Draco spoke slowly and melodically, taking time over each word and phrase. Celo wondered if his companion would even be able to tell an entire story that night, then realized he didn't much care.

"But the elements were alone and undefended, incapable of communicating with each other, snared within the matter that was theirs to control. And so, out of the endless void was created a race of guardians whose appointed task was to protect and defend the integrity of the four sacred elements. They were given powers, the better to fulfill their responsibilities; they were given strength and cunning and longevity to safeguard the treasures surrendered to their stewardship. To them alone would the elements respond. These guardians were—and are—dragons."

"You can command the elements?"

"If I so choose." Draco smiled, a slow curve that lifted the corner of his mouth.

"I thought you were enchanted."

"Compelled to take the form of one element until released. I chose earth, stone really, because I knew I could survive longer in the shelter of that element."

"Are you the last of your kind?" Celo had to ask, never having seen a dragon before. Gemma was a dragon shifter, but he hadn't seen her in her dragon form, and he'd never traveled to Incendium.

"I am the one of my kind, the only, the alpha and the omega." Draco glanced at Celo. "At least now."

"Then you're old."

"Old enough to remember the selection of Fiero-Four. Do you know why the system is called that?"

"Because there are four habitable planets in the system," Celo said, recalling his tutor's lessons.

Draco laughed and even the earth below him shook. "But you only live on two of them."

"It's true. Only Incendium and Regalia have cities, but Sylvawyld was used as a hunting ground." He left out the detail of his forebears hunting the verran to extinction there, as he doubted Draco would be impressed by that. "There aren't enough of us that we need to colonize Caligo."

"That's not the origin of the system's name," Draco said sternly.

"Then what is?"

"Fiero is a reference to fire, and four is a reference to the four dragons who came to this system. We weren't the first residents, but we brought knowledge and understanding and drew the inhabitants out of their dark ages." His eyes shone. "You could say we brought the spark of inspiration."

Celo sat up with interest. "Tell me what happened."

"I intended to, but you asked questions." There was a hint of censure in the dragon's tone, as well as enough amusement that Celo knew he was safe.

"I do apologize," he said, thinking it wise to be

particularly polite to a creature that could eat him in a single bite. "I'm just so interested."

"And so it is with people everywhere," Draco mused. "They are fascinated with dragons. Rightly so, to my thinking, given the splendor of our appearance and the extent of our powers."

"But I've never seen a dragon before."

Draco chuckled, making the mountain shake. "How many times have you looked at this mountain?"

"Every day."

The dragon turned slightly, the flames in his eyes dancing as he confronted Celo. "Then you've been looking at a dragon every day of your life. Just because you didn't realize as much doesn't mean I wasn't here." He lifted a brow. "Shall I tell the story?"

"Yes, please. I am sorry."

Draco exhaled, a long thread of smoke rising from each of his nostrils. The tendrils entwined as they rose into the night sky, creating a twisting pattern that was mesmerizing. It reminded Celo of two dragons tails tangling together. "And so it was that dragons were created, and so it was that they claimed this galaxy as their home."

"Fiero-Four isn't a galaxy..."

"We didn't originate here. Are you listening at all?"

"Of course."

"Do you know that every civilization that can see the cluster of stars of our home world has given it a name that refers to our kind? There is an awareness of our presence in the universe, in the dreams and visions of even those who have never seen us. In millions of cultures, we symbolize power, intelligence, and passion. And in all of those cultures, the fascination that people have for dragons is returned: dragons are equally fascinated with people."

Celo nodded and listened.

"We mate very seldom and offspring were always rare. They became increasingly rare as our numbers diminished. On our home world, we lost habitat to species that breed more quickly, whose numbers grow at rapid rates. As later became a pattern, we were hunted, for it was seen that we used many resources individually, resources that could instead support entire towns. We were attacked also for our hoards, our accumulations of material goods that give us pleasure, material goods that shine and sparkle and often are considered valuable by other species, too. Our numbers dwindled more quickly on our home world, so we colonized others.

"When the Fiero-Four system was deemed to possess suitable climactic conditions, we came here, to the planet that came to be known as Incendium. We were four in that first party, one for each element, as was the method of our colonization. In those days, Incendium was wild and lush, with bounty for all to share. Having learned the price of being outside the society of others, we mingled with the people here. We coexisted with them, proving ourselves useful, keeping our tempers in check, and for many eons, all was well.

"Perhaps it is the nature of coexistence, but the mutual interest of humans in dragons and dragons in humans began to find expression in passion. Princesses were brought to us as gifts, as homage, as trinkets to give us pleasure. No one should be surprised that dragons and damsels found methods of mating. The children of such unions inherited from father and mother, the most hardy combination being a son who took human form but once grown to manhood, could take dragon form, too.

"A dragon shifter," Celo breathed. "The Draconis Mutatus."

Draco nodded. "The first were not in command of their change. Like the werewolves of legend, these weredragons were subject to the influence of the elements. They might be commanded by the phase of the moon or sun, or the surge of desire within them. They were closer to beasts and struck terror into human hearts for their unpredictability. On Incendium, they were kept as pets."

"What happened to your three fellows?"

Draco visibly saddened. "I do not know. We lost the connection with each other. There was a great wave of revulsion for these weredragons in human society, because of their bursts of violence, which launched a familiar response. They were hunted and slaughtered, and we four strove to defend them as our offspring. Those who survived tried to hide their true nature, but often were unsuccessful. Still there were those humans who found the weredragons alluring, and sought them out, mating with them, creating yet more. The diminished proportion of dragon blood in these children stabilized the balance, but also cost many of them the ability to feel their fellows. We four lost our psychic connection with them."

"So, you couldn't defend them, because you couldn't find them."

Draco nodded. "And our bond with each other diminished, too. We disagreed on the course to follow and parted ways. It began with the one of us bound to the element of water. She had great empathy for all our descendants and could not bear to see them left to fend for themselves. She frequently risked her own welfare for others, and her silence made us fear she had been lost forever. Next, the one bound to the element of air disappeared from out awareness. Perhaps she was snared by a clever exchange of ideas, mixed with some enticing dreams. Perhaps she could not bear the thought of what we had become. The third and I retreated from human society together to ensure our own survival, but his connection was to fire. War drew him from the safety of our sanctuary and he could not resist a summons to defend our kind. I fear he may have died violently."

"Your affinity is with the earth," Celo guessed.

Draco nodded. "It gives me both patience and persistence, as well as the strength to wait a very long time. And so I was enchanted, by a young king who had no patience with my kind and no tolerance of my presence in the realm he sought to command."

"Surely you could have defeated him?"

"To what end? I was alone, separated from my kind or perhaps the last to survive. I was tired and feared a new age had dawned. I didn't want to die, but I didn't want to watch either. I let him enchant me."

"You let yourself be made powerless?"

Draco chuckled. "I've never been powerless. If I was, they would have built a city upon the flanks of the mountain I became. No, I knew that every spell can be broken, that it will be broken in time. I was prepared to wait. It is no accident that I became stone."

Celo nodded, understanding that Draco's affinity had both shaped the outcome of the spell and allowed him to survive it. "Tell me more about the shifters."

"As I said, over time, with the lineage of particularly bold human partners, the hybrid species stabilized. The addition of more humans to the mix meant that these shifters could change shape when they chose to do so. Their place in society changed then, as well—they became slaves instead of pets, their passion for their mates and kin used to keep them in check despite their greater physical strength."

"And they were fewer in number, too."

"Naturally. It was Scintillon who first rose in rebellion, having been provoked by an injustice done to a shifter and his kin, and Scintillon who was the first dragon king of Incendium. The great house of the kings of Incendium is founded upon the nobility and vigor of weredragon blood."

"You did know that he amounted to something!"

Draco chuckled. "I wasn't in a hurry to tell you everything I knew, and I was surprised by his success."

"Are the kings of Incendium your descendants?"

"They draw from the line of the dragon bound to air, which is why they sponsor science and invention. They are smitten with ideas and cleverness."

"But can you become a man?"

Draco shook his great head. "I am no weredragon. I was born of a dragon pair. I may be the last pure dragon to survive anywhere."

"The other three who colonized Fiero-Four were the same as you?"

Draco nodded. "We all originate in the same seed, though that was eons past. There are other anomalies that appeared over the ages, but first we must speak more of the shifters."

"On Incendium."

"Yes. For there, over time, the male gender became dominant. A child conceived by a weredragon and a human would be born male and a shifter, the vast majority of the time."

"But that can't be so," Celo protested. "King Ouros has twelve daughters."

Draco smiled. "We have not yet come to King Ouros and Queen Ignita. Our group of four was not the only team sent to colonize a planet. Dragons scattered though the universe in those dark days. Many lost track of each other as the eons passed, even with our long memories. Each local group mutated and adapted to its environment. Here in the Fiero-Four system, we remained aware of those dragon shifters on Excandesco and preserved relations with them."

"Queen Ignita's home planet."

"And there, the opposite situation developed. The

female became the most likely gender of any child conceived by a dragon shifter and human. The ascendant line is from the founder allied with fire, so they are passionate and emotional dragon shifters. Just as the presence of air feeds a flame, I am certain that Ignita and Ouros have a fiery match."

"Is it true that they don't let the human partner survive after the mating on Excandesco?"

"It is. Although the mating is seen as valuable and imperative, the human male is regarded to be inferior and unnecessary once the seed has been delivered and the child conceived. Those dragon queens are ferocious in their conviction, and tolerate no possible threat to their rule."

"Was Ouros an exception because he was a dragon shifter, too?"

"That could be so. I do not know the pair, only their history. It is not surprising that they had to flee Excandesco to live together, and it shouldn't be surprising either that the introduction of Queen Ignita's heritage into the lineage of Incendium meant more daughters than sons."

"It seems they shouldn't be all sons."

Draco placed another log upon the fire, lifting it easily into place despite its size. "That might have something to do with the curse."

Chapter Two

The curse?" Celo had never heard about a curse placed upon the house of Incendium, much less one upon dragons. "What curse?"

The dragon sighed. "Let us talk of the triumph of Scintillon first. Those who believed him to be a usurper were exiled to Regalia, which had previously been unoccupied, and rebellion bred on this planet ever after." Draco blinked. "I liked it here before the exile. It was quiet."

"It's no accident that Regalia was kept in a primitive state," Celo noted. "We were not trusted with technology."

"Your forbears did not want it," Draco noted. "They wanted magic."

Celo knew that was true.

"And when the population was divided between Incendium and Regalia, each group charted their own course. The dragon shifters of Incendium, and all those who lived beneath their control, looked to the stars for inspiration and for their quests. They developed the means of traveling in space, raising the standard of living and education level of all their citizens. They fostered research, development, and the analysis of their world. They became scientists, shining the light of knowledge and reason on mysteries yet to be explained."

"They followed the impulse of their forebear, the dragon governed by the element of air," Celo said and Draco nodded with approval.

"Excellent. Yes, Celo, they did." He raised a talon and continued his tale. "Those on Regalia, in contrast, turned to the darkness. They sought truth in mystery, in the secrets of the earth and the shadows of the heart and soul. They studied the arcane and embraced that which could not be readily explained. They became spell casters and augury readers, people who listened to their instincts and found truth echoed in their surroundings." Draco eyed Celo, his orange eyes glowing. "They learned the language of birds and beasts. They taught themselves how to cast dreams and read thoughts and influence the actions of those beyond their reach. They became magicians."

"Scientists and magicians. Do you mean to say one is better than the other?" Celo asked, his pride pricked.

Draco laughed. "On the contrary, my princely friend, they are two sides of the same coin. Light and dark. Science and magic. Knowledge and instinct." He held Celo's gaze as if that was important, but Celo couldn't guess why. "Both rooted in the same element."

"Air!"

"Air," Draco agreed. "What do you think that means?"

"That there really should be more unions like that of Venero and Gemma, for Regalia and Incendium should become one kingdom again. The light and the dark should be gathered again into the whole."

"Precisely," Draco agreed.

"I could take that message to Venero. He'd see it as a challenge and an opportunity, a goal for his reign."

"Good," Draco said and fell silent. After a moment, he cleared his throat and looked over Regalia again, his thoughts veiled. The sky was getting quite dark, and Celo could see stars overhead. It would have been very chilly without the fire, which still burned steadily. The light glowed on Draco's scales and sparks danced upward from the blaze. The heat was making Celo a little sleepy, but he knew Draco hadn't finished his story. He could sense the dragon mustering his words.

Or choosing them.

"There must be more," he prompted finally.

"More?"

"A plan or a quest. It is a fine enough tale, but it's not much of a reward."

Draco chuckled a little. "You aren't the spellbreaker."

"But I'm here and I'm listening," Celo countered. "What about the curse? What affected the dragon shifters of Excandesco?"

"I told you that our kind left our home in groups of four."

"That one in each group had an affinity to each element, yes, and that you were all dragons bred of dragons."

"I didn't tell you why we left."

"You said you were hunted."

"But we were hunted because we were perceived to be weakening."

"Why?" Celo couldn't imagine thinking of a dragon as weak, especially one as massive as Draco.

"We became cursed with infertility amongst our own kind. It was after a...dispute with the High Priestess of Nimue."

"What kind of dispute?"

"A dispute I'm not at liberty to share with you," Draco replied somewhat tersely. "*That's* not my story."

"Can you tell me the result of the curse?"

"Of course. Offspring had always been rare but they became almost non-existent. We live long but are not immortal, and there was fear that our kind might become extinct if we didn't act."

Celo nodded understanding.

"Did anyone talk to the High Priestess?"

"She wasn't known for listening to dissenting views. Probably still isn't."

Celo didn't know. He'd never heard much about her beyond her name.

Draco cleared his throat. "We left our home planet in search of new possibilities, and also in the hope of establishing legacies elsewhere in the universe. So many of us established dynasties of dragon shifters that our kind are known in every civilization. But there was divisiveness before we embarked upon our quest, and we became more different from each other than similar." Draco exhaled smoke, considering this. "Perhaps that was the true root of our infertility. We had become strangers to ourselves."

"I don't know nearly enough about dragons, it appears. Are there more differences than being connected with one of the four elements?"

"Not originally, but change came. Those allied with the element of air because mist dragons, fog dragons, cloud dragons, guardians of spirits, dreams, and inspiration. Those allied with the element of earth became mountain dragons, earth dragons, beach dragons, guardians of stones, riches, and material wealth. Those allied with water became sea dragons, rain dragons, and snow dragons, guardians of weather, emotion, and empathy. Those allied with fire became war dragons, fiery dragons, light dragons, guardians of passion, power, and persistence. And within each of the four kinds, there was the separation of light and dark as well."

Celo was rapt. "Did mating only occur with the same kind and inclination, or did opposites attract?"

"We thought there had to be a union of differences, but it's possible that we were mistaken. The four of us who came to Fiero-Four, despite our efforts, did not breed with our own kind. The only offspring were from union of the mist dragon in our number with the humans of Incendium."

"So you have no children of any kind?"

Draco shook his head. "Not personally, but we four all considered those children that resulted from the mist dragon's unions to be our own. We consider all with dragon blood to be our kin."

Celo reasoned that if the lineage of the pure dragons was tracked, there had to be a relationship, however distant, between those four founding dragons. "What did the mates of the mist dragon bring to the union?"

Draco was dismissive. "Who can say? I barely remember them."

But surely someone did?

Draco raised a talon. "The dragon of greater import, at least to me," he continued. "Once we were numerous." His voice boomed. "Once we celebrated the variety of our kind. But as our numbers dwindled and we scattered in search of refuge and opportunity, we became as solitary fragments, each of us only carrying a small measure of the wisdom of our kind." Draco smiled down at Celo. "We are old beyond old. We have memories that stretch back through the ages. But even that has limitations. I remember the lore of the light-seeking earth dragons, which would only be an eighth of the truth, if I remembered it all."

"You need to bring all the dragons back together again."

"Someone must."

"But you think the other dragons are dead or lost."

"I know they are not on Regalia. That again is only part of the truth."

"Then where are they? Did they survive?"

"I do not know. Seeking them is not my task."

"I don't understand."

The massive dragon smiled. "That quest is your reward, Prince Celo of Regalia. That is why the raven sent you, because he knew you were the one destined to gather all the dragons of old together again."

"Actually, it was the owl who knew that," Celo clarified.

"There is great wisdom in the creatures of the wild. Your ability to understand them perhaps makes you a good choice for this task."

"But that doesn't mean I can find dragons," Celo protested. "If they still exist. I can't hear your thoughts at all..."

"Are you afraid to pursue your destiny?"

"No, but..."

"To leave Regalia? Has your life here been filled with such joy as that?"

Celo frowned. He'd never left Regalia and never imagined that he would. He hadn't been particularly happy on this planet, not after his mother's abuse, but his solution had been to retreat into the forest—not to venture to the stars in pursuit of dragons.

He'd done as Draco indicated, looking to the earth instead of the sky for a solution.

Celo had known from birth that he'd never travel beyond Fiero-Four, as only those on Incendium had the ability to travel to other worlds. In fact, he wouldn't be able to even get to Incendium without help from Incendium and he wouldn't get to Incendium's starport easily. He had a hundred objections to Draco's plan within seconds.

"I don't even know anybody on Incendium," he protested. "I think you have the wrong prince. My brother Venero would be a better choice, since he married into the Incendium royal family."

"So, you do know someone from Incendium. It

seems to me that, from your recollection, Queen Gemma might owe you a favor."

"But Venero..."

"Is surely very busy as king of the realm."

There was that.

And really, Celo had so many objections that he had to give the idea serious consideration. Was he afraid?

What if he *did* embark on this quest? What if he did seek dragons?

He had to think that women would find that interesting.

He was pretty curious himself. What had happened to the dragons? What had been the dispute with the High Priestess of Nimue? Could that curse be broken by bringing the dragons together again? Or would it take even more?

He looked at Draco, then at the burning fire. "How exactly do I find dragons?"

"How did you find me?"

The raven, Celo thought. *I need to take Nix with me.*

"A most sensible plan," Draco said aloud. "There *is* more to you than meets the eye."

Despite himself, Celo found his excitement rising. Any of the other three dragons who had first come to Fiero-Four might think that Draco was dead, after all, since he'd been enchanted for so long. Where might they be?

Was it a coincidence that four dragons had come to a system with four inhabitable planets?

Would he find the other two on Sylvawyld or Caligo?

If they were disguised, their affinity with an element would have to hold a clue. Perhaps one was a lake or another was a blizzard. Maybe one was a fire that wouldn't die.

He would first seek the mist dragon who Draco said was the forebear of the dragon shifters of Incendium. He had to think that she might still be somewhere on Incendium, watching over her own descendants.

"Now you're thinking," Draco rumbled with approval.

Maybe, after he'd found Fiero-Four's founding dragons, he'd have to go to Excandesco and look for *their* founding dragons. Maybe it was the same, that only one of those four had managed to produce offspring that were shifters. Maybe he could find the fire dragon and learn more.

And then there was Nimue.

"How many groups of four dragons were there?"

"I remember four," Draco said, leaning his chin upon his foreleg. He sighed so that a shudder rolled through his body from snout to tail, then his eyes began to close.

"Do you know where the other two groups went?"

"Not anymore."

"When I find them, where are they supposed to meet? And when?"

"That is for you to resolve, Prince Celo."

"And what will they do? How will they share their knowledge with each other and with everyone else?"

Draco opened one eye. "You have far too many questions."

"You don't have enough answers."

The dragon smiled. "Why else would there be a quest?" He nudged another branch toward the fire and sparks flew into the night sky as the fire seized the new fuel. He yawned then, his jaw creaking and his tongue unfurling. Celo had a good look at all those teeth and the wet red cave that led down the dragon's gullet. "Sleep now. I will take you as far as Regalia's main city in the morning."

"So long as we stop for the raven on the way," Celo stipulated.

Draco opened one eye. "Well, this is progress. First

you were terrified of me and now you're making demands."

Celo smiled. "I'm not going to succeed at a quest by sitting back and waiting for it to happen."

"No, you're not." Draco's eyes closed and his breathing deepened. It seemed to Celo that the dragon almost turned back into a mountain. Draco's breath was so slow that Celo could barely see the dragon's chest fill. It took what seemed like an eternity for him to inhale and even longer for him to exhale. The fire crackled and burned, and the stars spun overhead. It was warm and he felt that curious mix of exhaustion and excitement.

A quest.

He could hardly wait to begin.

There were shouts in the bailey at midday and Venero left the audience chamber of the palace to find out what was amiss. Gemma hurried after him, her curiosity clear. They were both dressed practically, as if they meant to ride to battle. Gemma wasn't inclined to wear queenly attire and Venero didn't mind that she looked like a warrior princess all the time.

They had been working hard together to rebuild the fortunes of Regalia and to win the trust of its residents. They had made progress but there was a great deal still to be done.

"Dragon!" cried the sentinel. "Dragon attack!"

Venero captured Gemma's hand and they raced into the courtyard together just as there was whoosh of wind overhead. Venero caught a glimpse of a massive scaled belly just overhead and Gemma reached for her bow. The guards loosed a volley of arrows but they bounced off the dragon's scales and clattered to the ground.

The dragon roared, shooting a plume of fire into the air as it turned in the distance. It was a massive creature, much bigger than Gemma and her family were in their dragon forms.

"A dragon," Gemma whispered, sniffing the air. She caught Venero's questioning glance and guessed his thoughts. "Not a shifter. Not like me."

"Just dragon?"

"Maybe *all* dragon would be more accurate." She stepped into the open fearlessly and took a deep breath. "So old," she whispered in awe. "So large. It's a legend come to life."

Venero didn't quite share his wife's wonder.

The dragon beat his wings hard and flew directly toward the castle again. Women screamed and children were rushed into buildings for safety even though they obviously would have preferred to watch.

"To arms!" Venero cried, wondering how they could defend themselves against such a creature. Everything looked flimsy in comparison to its strength and he'd already seen that arrows were useless.

Gemma put aside her bow and began to shimmer blue.

"No!" Venero cried, but Gemma shifted shape, taking her dragon form before his very eyes. Her scales were a deep blue and they glittered in the winter sunlight. Her chest was gold and she looked like a jeweled ornament in comparison to the massive dragon as grey as weathered stone.

"Hold your fire!" Venero cried, fearing that his queen was taking too much of a chance. Gemma launched herself into the air.

The others on the ground watched, mesmerized, as the dragons approached each other. Venero was certain that his wasn't the only mouth that was dry.

The large dragon circled around Gemma, making her look as small as a butterfly beside him. He seemed to be as intrigued by her as she was by him.

Was the other dragon laughing?

He breathed a torrent of fire straight up into the sky that seemed somehow joyous, then Gemma did the same. They could have been dancing together in the sky, Gemma flying around him as he turned back toward the castle again.

The orange flame in his eyes was anything but playful, though. Venero's fears for his people and his queen were renewed. What could they do?

"Venero!" someone shouted.

It sounded like Celo. But where was Celo? As far as Venero knew, his brother was still in the forests, living as a hermit far from the capital city. He scanned the crowd that had gathered to watch the mighty dragon, hoping to spot his brother.

He didn't.

So, he opened his mind.

Look up! Celo cried, more triumphant and excited than Venero had ever heard him. *I'm riding a dragon!*

What does he want from us?

Nothing. He's giving me a ride!

The large dragon bore down on the castle and the bowsmen raised their weapons again.

"Hold your fire!" Venero shouted once more, fearing that more could be lost than gained. He could see someone perched between the dragon's horns, holding on with one hand and waving the other. "It's Prince Celo!"

His guards stood down, but their expressions remained wary as the massive dragon hovered beside the castle. His wings made a fierce wind and Venero had to cover his eyes to protect them from the swirling dust. The dragon stretched down and rested his chin upon the ground, then Celo walked down his snout to the ground.

He turned back to give the dragon a pat. "Thanks, Draco. I'll be back as soon as I can."

"I'll be waiting," the dragon rumbled, his words

making the ground shake. His bright gaze fixed on Venero, a burning stare that seemed to be filled with fire.

Gemma landed in the courtyard and shifted shape, her action drawing Draco's gaze. His eyes glittered as he watched her and there was no doubt that he smiled.

Gemma bowed before him. "Thank you, Draco," she said, that wonder still in his tone.

Draco nodded, then lifted his head. He beat his wings so hard that the water in the river rose after him. He flew high in the sky then turned to the south.

They stood as one in silence watching until his silhouette faded from view.

"Where did he come from?" Venero asked when Celo came closer. His brother's clothes were worse for wear, his boots worn out and his cloak dirty. His beard was longer and his face was tanned, but his eyes were filled with such enthusiasm that he almost looked like a stranger.

Venero couldn't remember Celo being so excited about anything.

"That's Mount Draco," Celo said with a grin. "He's an earth dragon and probably heading back to sleep."

Venero exchanged a glance with Gemma.

"A real dragon," she said and Celo nodded. "I didn't think there were any real dragons, not anymore." She stared after Draco, and Venero wondered if she could still see him with her keen dragon gaze.

"Neither did I," his brother agreed. "But Draco wants me to look for them. He gave me a quest, and I'm going to take it." He glanced back at the whistle of smaller wings and everyone watched a raven fly directly to Celo. It landed on his shoulder, its wings gleaming blue-black and they nodded to each other, then looked at Venero as one.

"Nix and I need to go to Incendium," Celo said. "We're both hungry, too, and I could use some new clothes. Introductions on Incendium, too."

Venero smiled. It was so good to see his brother with purpose. "When I said you could ask me for anything, I didn't think you would," he teased.

"Oh, this is just the start," Celo said. "After Incendium, I'm going to need to go to Sylvawyld and Caligo."

"No one goes to Caligo," Venero noted.

"That's going to change," Celo said. "Then Excandesco."

"Is that all?" Venero asked with a smile.

"And after that?" Gemma asked.

"No idea, but I'm sure I'll need more favors." Celo grinned, confident that Venero would help him. The bird nodded, its black eyes shining, and Venero found himself laughing.

"It can't be a coincidence that you arrived just in time for lunch."

"Not at all."

"What happens when you find the dragons?"

"I don't know, but I have a feeling it'll shake things up." At Venero's gesture of invitation, the three of them turned to go into the castle. Venero could smell the roast meat being carried to the dining hall and he smiled when Celo's stomach grumbled.

"I'm starving," he murmured and the bird croaked agreement. "It's a good thing Draco flies as fast as he does."

A pretty servant brought a basin of water for Celo—two others brought basins for Venero and Gemma—and he smiled at her as he washed up. "You rode a dragon," she breathed in awe.

"I did! It was a bit bumpy at first, but a great ride." He turned to Venero. "Which reminds me, you need to build more connections between Regalia and Incendium. Draco explained to me that our future lies in cooperation."

"That's exactly what we believe," Venero said, escorting Gemma to the table. "All suggestions welcome."

Celo smiled. "Advice from a dragon is fair exchange for all the help I'm going to ask of you."

"I'll take you to Incendium myself," Gemma said as they were seated. She patted her stomach. "I need to visit my mother's physician and have the baby's charts cast."

"And you're going to take a Starpod," Venero said, feeling gruff and protective. He'd talk to her in private about her impulsive dragon flight. He didn't want to think about the risk she'd already taken, but he'd keep her from taking more. "You're not going to fly to Incendium under your own power. I don't care how adept you are at casting an orb, never mind that you'd have Celo to look after as well." The raven croaked. "And Nix."

Gemma gave him a sunny smile. "Dragons are supposed to be the protective ones," she teased, then eyed Celo. "Is that why he gave you a mission? To protect us all?"

"And to find all the dragons again, bring them together, and preserve the knowledge they've gathered." The meal was served and they began to eat, even as Celo shared what Draco had told him. Venero didn't know if it was all the dragon had confided in his brother, but there were plenty of suggestions that he could use to bring the two kingdoms closer.

Never mind that Celo had a glow of purpose that was new and welcome.

He smiled at Gemma, thinking that dragons were proving to be very good luck for Regalia—and that despite the fact that the kingdom had been founded out of a protest against the dragon king of Incendium.

There was no doubt that Celo had been changed by his encounter with Draco. He stood taller, he voiced his opinion more readily, and he was filled with confidence. Women in the castle and its surrounds noticed, and there were already whispers about the prince who had become a dragon hunter. Venero wondered what else Celo would find on his quest.

He couldn't wait to find out.

The next morning, Princess Bellatora, Mistress of the Hunt, was striding through the starport of Incendium with her younger sister, Flammara. They were scheduled to depart for Terra to visit Drakina and Troy, and to assess the hunting for their father. Were the wild boars of Terra as similar to the extinct verran of Sylvawyld as Drakina insisted? Bellatora was assigned to find out.

Unfortunately, she was also supposed to take her younger sister with her. She was already wishing that part would end.

"You'll enjoy it," she said to her reluctant younger sister for the hundredth time. "You've always wanted to have an adventure. Now that you're being offered one, all you can do is complain."

"I'm not complaining," Flammara replied tartly. "Just making an observation."

Bellatora wished it could have been just one observation.

Actually, it was one, she realized, but Flammara was making the same observation over and over and over again. It was enough to make her itch for her bow.

Or a mace.

Bellatora might have been born female, but most of the time she felt that she understood men much better than women.

"And pouting," she continued. "You're definitely pouting." She said this as if it were a crime, and to Bellatora, it might as well have been. Nothing was achieved by pouting, in her view.

"I am *not* pouting." Flammara stood taller and tossed her hair. More than one starpilot turned to watch the sisters pass. "I'm *furious.*"

"With Father?"

"Of course, with Father! He's only sending me with you because he wants me away from Thierry."

Bellatora sighed, suspecting that was true and knowing that Flammara would never see the value of that. "Maybe he's just trying to protect you."

"Maybe he's standing in the path of true love!"

Bellatora barely refrained from rolling her eyes. True love had nothing to do with it. The last thing that would ever affect Thierry, a knight in her father's service and a popular champion, was affection for another person. That man loved himself above all else, and she disliked how Thierry encouraged Flammara's interest in him.

She didn't need dragon vision to see the knight's true ambitions.

"He should never have worn your colors in that tournament," she said beneath her breath, knowing how her sister would reply.

"But he did! And he *won*! And it was completely romantic."

"It was calculated," Bellatora snapped, her patience expiring. "You have to see that. Thierry is concerned with his own comfort and thinks that marrying into the royal family would be the best choice for his future."

"If that's so, why hasn't he ever shown interest in any of you?"

"Maybe we're too smart to fall for his ruse."

"Oh! I can't believe you would think such things about a man pledged to Father's service, an honorable champion..."

Bellatora ignored her sister's chatter. They were passing a bay where a Starpod was docking. She absently checked the displayed registration and realized it was from Regalia. She inhaled and knew that her sister Gemma was aboard, if not the pilot.

That would make sense. It had to be about the right time to consult with Mother's doctor about the baby. It was a good idea for her to use a Starpod rather than flying herself and spinning an orb in her condition. Bellatora nodded with approval, not at all surprised that her older sister was so practical and logical about pregnancy.

Flammara, on the other hand, would be whimsical and emotional...

Bellatora stopped in her tracks. She breathed deeply, letting a beguiling scent fill her lungs and send heat through her entire body. It made her shimmer. It made her tingle.

It made her yearn.

She pivoted slowly, oblivious to Flammara, and eyed the dock of the Starpod from Regalia.

The Seed.

Gemma had, by accident or design, brought Bellatora's Carrier of the Seed to Incendium. Her heart began to pound in anticipation.

"Bellatora!" Flammara cried. "We'll be late. Come on!"

"Go without me," Bellatora said, walking toward the gate, drawn toward her destiny like a fish on a line.

"What? I can't go without you. Father said..."

"It's the Seed," Bellatora whispered with vigor and Flammara felt silent. "Father will understand perfectly. Go!" She stopped and held her breath, watching hungrily as the portal swung wide.

• • •

Look for
Wyvern's Angel

Book 9 in the Dragons of Incendium series

The Dragons of Incendium have their own website
http://dragonsofincendium.com

Books by Deborah Cooke

Paranormal Romances:
The Dragonfire Series
Kiss of Fire
Kiss of Fury
Kiss of Fate
Harmonia's Kiss
Winter Kiss
Whisper Kiss
Darkfire Kiss
Flashfire
Ember's Kiss
Kiss of Danger
Kiss of Darkness
Kiss of Destiny
Serpent's Kiss
Firestorm Forever

The Dragons of Incendium
Wyvern's Mate
Nero's Dream
Wyvern's Prince
Arista's Legacy
Wyvern's Warrior
Kraw's Secret
Wyvern's Outlaw
Celo's Quest
Wyvern's Angel
Nimue's Gift

Paranormal Young Adult:
The Dragon Diaries
Flying Blind
Winging It
Blazing the Trail

Urban Fantasy Romance
The Prometheus Project
Fallen
Guardian
Rebel
Abyss

Deborah Cooke sold her first book in 1992, a medieval romance called **The Romance of the Rose** published under her pseudonym Claire Delacroix. Since then, she has published over fifty novels in a wide variety of sub-genres, including historical romance, contemporary romance, paranormal romance, fantasy romance, time-travel romance, women's fiction, paranormal young adult and fantasy with romantic elements. She has published under the names Claire Delacroix, Claire Cross, and Deborah Cooke. **The Beauty**, part of her successful Bride Quest series of historical romances, was her first title to land on the *New York Times* List of Bestselling Books. Her books routinely appear on other bestseller lists and have won numerous awards. In 2009, she was the writer-in-residence at the Toronto Public Library, the first time the library has hosted a residency focused on the romance genre. In 2012, she was honored to receive the Romance Writers of America's Mentor of the Year Award.

Currently, she writes paranormal romances and contemporary romances under the name Deborah Cooke. She also writes medieval romances as Claire Delacroix. Deborah lives in Canada with her husband and family, as well as far too many unfinished knitting projects.

For more information about Deborah's books,
please visit her website at

http://deborahcooke.com